Sign up for our newsletter to hear
about new and upcoming releases.

www.ylva-publishing.com

# Hold My Hand

 AC OSWALD

# Chapter 1

SAVANNAH TURNED THE KEY IN the lock to her front door. Her hand shook. She straightened her jacket and carefully stepped inside, trying not to make any noise.

She tiptoed to the kitchen and switched on the light.

"Who is she?"

"Jesus, Bethany, you scared the shit out of me!"

Bethany leaned against the kitchen counter, her eyes red rimmed and puffy. She looked as tired as fuck.

Savannah knew that her next words would seal the fate of their relationship. Truth or lie? Either way, Bethany was going to get hurt.

"Seriously, Savy. Tell me her name. I want to know." Bethany sounded so powerless, as if she had already given up the fight.

A fist in her jacket pocket just barely kept her hand from shaking. She swallowed back a lump in her throat. "Lory," she said. "Her name's Lory. Loredana, actually. She's Italian."

Hurt simmered in Bethany's eyes. She looked like she'd been punched in the stomach.

"Isn't that what you expected to hear?" Savannah asked.

For a while, no one said anything, and the silence became suffocating.

"Do you want me to leave?" Savannah tried to keep her gaze steady. She had just thrown away five years, five long, happy years together.

Bethany picked up her shoes and put on her jacket over her old Mickey Mouse sweatshirt and pajama pants.

"Where are you going, Beth?" Savannah's gaze followed Beth's every movement.

"I'll go to my mom's place for now, I guess," Bethany whispered. She removed the hair tie from her ponytail, and the strands cascaded onto her face.

Savannah knew this was so she wouldn't see her tears. She saw them anyway.

"I'm sorry, Beth. I really am." She sighed. "You deserve better."

Bethany's head snapped up. "I deserve better?" She let out a sarcastic laugh. "Just tell me why. I want a reason, okay? Then I'm out."

What to tell her? There was no way she could give her the real reason. She had made her decision, and there was no turning back.

"It's not you, it's me." Wow. What a cliché.

Bethany shook her head. "You can't even give me a real reason. Don't you think I deserve that much?"

She did deserve that much. She deserved all the good things in the world. Bethany was the most kind-hearted, funny, beautiful, loving person Savannah had ever met. Which was why all this was for the best.

"You're right," Savannah said. "It's just that I realized..." Her throat closed over. "I realized I moved on, okay? This is not what I want. I don't want to spend the rest of my life with you in this apartment." It was hard to keep her voice even. "I don't want to have kids. I need space." She felt evil speaking those words when she saw the effect they had on the one person who meant the world to her.

"Space to spend time with your Italian chick?" Bethany mopped her tears with her sleeve. "I'm sorry my pizza sucked."

Savannah couldn't bear it any longer. She leaned against the fridge, her eyes shut. "Maybe it's best if you leave now."

She tried to focus on her breathing. This would soon be over. She'd let Bethany leave, and then she'd move on; she'd somehow make it. She'd somehow manage alone. It was for the best—at least the best for Bethany—and Savannah needed to remember that.

The door clicked closed. First the kitchen door, then the front door. Then the apartment fell silent.

In the silence, she finally could let loose. Tears streamed down her face, and she sank to the floor, punching the linoleum next to her.

This was what she had wanted, what she had planned. It was the only way to get out of their relationship. It *had* to be this way.

"*Stay strong,*" she told herself and fumbled through her bag. She pulled out a small bottle of pills and poured two into her palm.

"Fuck this shit," she said aloud and swallowed the pills, blinking away tears that refused to stop. "Fuck this shit."

A year later and Bethany still asked herself what she had done wrong.

Sometimes it didn't feel like a year. Sometimes it felt as if they had kissed only yesterday.

They had not spoken since that night Savannah broke up with her. Bethany had picked up her stuff while Savannah was at work. She left her key on the kitchen table. She had wanted to leave a note but hadn't known what to say:

Please change your mind.

Whatever I did, I'm sorry.

You're mean, Savannah. Mean. Here's your stupid key.

I hope you'll be happy with her.

I could have learned how to make better pizza. You should have told me.

Call me, please.

In the end, she had ripped up the would-be note and stuffed it into her jeans pocket. What was there to say on such a small piece of paper? What *could* she say after such a long relationship?

Bethany knew she wasn't the smartest person in the world, but she was an expert on Savannah Cortez. She knew how to analyze Savy's emotions, her actions, her words. But for a while before their breakup, Savannah had become distant and cool, and Bethany had become confused.

Leaving early and coming home late had become routine with Savannah. She never said where she was going, and she seemed to have lost all of her happiness. Bethany had known something was wrong, but whenever she tried to talk it out, Savannah closed up.

What had made Savannah do it? Why cheat with someone else?

Even after all this time, not knowing the answers drove Bethany nuts. And now, even with a new girlfriend in her life, she couldn't stop thinking about Savannah.

She was happy with Amber, her new girl. Amber was nice, pretty, friendly. A sweetheart, really. But all these images, all these questions, all these unresolved feelings—they still hadn't left her head.

She and Amber didn't live together, and Bethany didn't think she wanted to take that step anytime soon. Trusting someone new wasn't easy, even though Bethany tended to see only the good in people. But then, where had trust gotten her? She'd had her heart broken. Badly. And as much as she tried to deny it, the break with Savannah had taken away *her* happiness. The world had felt gray. With one conversation, all her plans for the future had been erased.

Then, two months ago in July, Amber became a new client at the salon Bethany had started working at. They'd started chatting about miserable dates during one appointment, and Bethany had almost dropped her scissors when Amber started talking about dating a woman with a fetish for fake moustaches. They both started laughing uncontrollably. It had been a long time since Bethany had felt so lighthearted. One week later, she and Amber met for dinner, which led to sex, which led to more dates. It had been easy, especially since Amber and Savannah couldn't have been more different.

Bethany tried to ignore how much she missed snuggling with Savannah on the couch. Or linking pinkies when they went shopping for groceries. Or being pulled into a protective hug whenever they watched a silly horror movie.

She and Amber hadn't even had a real fight yet. Sure, there had been small disagreements, but at some point, Amber would smile and tell her they should just forget about it and that it would be okay. With Savannah, there had been countless fights. Was it ridiculous to miss fighting, to miss the look Savannah would give her when she had done something wrong? She missed the way Savannah would carefully approach her from behind and position a shy kiss on her cheek as an apology.

Was it ridiculous to still think about the many times they had danced in the kitchen together, waiting for their pasta to cook? To smile when she thought about how dorky they must have looked, hopping around? Savannah would push her against the kitchen counter and kiss her until she felt dizzy. Those kisses were why they ate burnt pasta most nights.

4

Amber never burned the pasta. She worked in catering and knew how to prepare a perfect dinner. Their relationship was nice, nothing anyone could complain about.

Was Savannah still dating this Lory chick? At first, she had wanted to track down all the Loredanas in the city to see what the "other woman" was like but then had decided against it.

"You okay?" The question finally woke Bethany from her little trance.

"Sure." She attempted a smile. "Why wouldn't I be?"

Amber gave her a weird look and pointed at the cone in Bethany's hand and the chocolate ice cream that was running down her fingers.

"Oh."

She handed Bethany a napkin and helped her clean up the mess.

"You're such a child sometimes." She dabbed at a smear of ice cream on the tip of Bethany's nose.

Bethany smiled, wiped her nose, and took Amber's hand in hers. They continued their walk through the park. It was one of the last warm September days, and the leaves had started changing their color. It was a pretty afternoon with her pretty girlfriend. Bethany figured she should be happy.

The salon wasn't exactly the hippest place in town, but Bethany loved seeing a lot of friendly faces there every day. The clientele were mostly housewives, some elderly ladies, and children.

Mrs. McClary's hair was resting in the curling iron when the door jangled open and she heard the receptionist say, "Miss Cortez, it's been a while. What can we do for you?"

Bethany froze. In the mirror, she saw Savannah talking to Anna at the reception desk.

"Ouch," Mrs. McClary complained. Bethany had grazed her ear with the hot iron.

"Oh God, I'm so sorry," she mumbled. Her hands were shaking. She risked another look into the mirror and made eye contact with Savannah, who looked equally as shocked.

Savannah's gaze darted away and then fell back on Bethany again in less than a moment, as if she were trying to decide whether or not to turn and run.

"Miss Cortez?"

Savannah visibly startled. "Uh," she stuttered, "you know what? Um, I'll come back some other time. I...I'm sorry."

She turned on her heel, gave Anna an apologetic look, and headed for the exit.

"Excuse me for a minute." Bethany dropped the curling iron and ran after Savannah. There was no time to think about her actions. Pure instinct made her follow before it was too late. She didn't know what she wanted to say, but she needed to look at her for a few seconds more. She needed to see an up close reaction to their meeting. She needed...anything but to see her turn her back and go.

"Savannah! Wait, please!"

The glass door closed behind her, and they stood in the street, staring at each other.

Savannah broke their gaze first. She looked down at the asphalt.

"Savy, it's...it's been a while." Bethany tried to smile.

"Yeah," Savannah replied. "How are you doing, Beth?"

This was beyond weird.

Bethany wasn't sure what she was feeling, if it was excitement or sadness coursing through her body. She was surprised to feel no anger. Somehow the anger had vanished in the past year. Now all she saw was a person she used to love. She needed to be around her for a little while longer.

"I'm fine. Good. Great, actually," Bethany babbled, laughing excitedly. "I have a job here. It's nice."

"I can see that," Savannah said. "Much better than that cheap salon at the mall, eh?"

Bethany nodded. She had to resist the urge to reach for Savannah's hand.

"You look great." Savannah's face had gone more serious, and Bethany knew she meant it.

"Thanks. You look..." Her gaze travelled up and down Savannah's body, and she couldn't help but frown.

"Hot?" Savannah asked, but Beth only frowned.

"I was going to say 'thin,' but..." Savannah had lost a lot of weight since she'd last seen her.

"Rice diet." Savannah shrugged and pressed her bag close to her belly.

"How are things with..."

"Lory?" Savannah asked in a tone that Bethany couldn't interpret.

"Yeah, Lory. So, how's things with you?"

"Everything's great. I mean… I don't know. I guess it's still awkward to talk about it, don't you think?" Savannah mumbled. Her gaze didn't meet Bethany's.

"No, it's fine. I mean, I'm glad to hear you're happy. And I'm happy too. I found someone new, and she's fun to be around, and…yeah. I have nothing to complain about."

The smile was still frozen on Savannah's lips, but her gaze softened. "I'm really glad to hear that, Beth," she said through halting breaths. She sounded sincere. "You deserve to be happy."

She reached out to cover Bethany's hand with her own and squeezed it tightly. For a second, Bethany thought she could see a tear in Savannah's eyes. Then Savannah's hand was gone from hers.

"I'm on my way to see Lory right now." Savannah fiddled with her long, dark curls. "But it was nice seeing you again."

Bethany's heart pounded faster as something like panic washed over her. She didn't want to say good-bye to Savannah again without knowing if she'd ever see her again. It was silly to ask her to stay, to ask for her number. She didn't even know what she wanted from her—friendship? All she knew was that she didn't want Savannah to go.

"Can we hang out sometime?" She hated the desperate tone in her voice. "Maybe for a coffee? Or a hot chocolate?"

Why did she have to look so tortured? Savannah bit her lower lip and sighed. "I don't know, Beth. I—"

"Only to talk about good old times, Savy. I know you're in a relationship. I am too. I don't want anything from you, okay? Just… I want to hear what you've been up to." Bethany toyed with the zipper of her shirt. "I missed you. I mean… I miss being your friend. We've always been best friends," she added in a whisper.

"Okay." Savannah kicked at a nonexistent rock on the sidewalk. "I guess a coffee seems fine."

A loud sigh coursed through Bethany. "My cell's still the same." She smiled. "If you still have the number."

"I know it by heart," Savannah admitted with a shy smile. "I mean, it's an easy number. Many threes, not so hard."

Bethany smiled and brushed her hand along Savannah's arm. "I'll be waiting for your call," she said softly before she turned and ran back to poor Mrs. McClary.

When she went back inside, she glanced into the mirror. She was *red*, red as a tomato. Her head felt as if it were on fire, yet somehow she felt happy. And yet somehow she also had to fight back the tears. Even after all this time, Savannah hadn't changed. She was still so damn confusing.

Savannah finally arrived at her destination. She had tried to remain calm, had tried not to let the unexpected encounter with Bethany drive her nuts. She had managed to avoid Bethany for such a long time and thought she was almost over her. After so long apart, she had hoped she could finally be strong without her. How could seeing her still hurt so much after all this time?

Why, oh why did Beth have to start working in that stupid salon? She certainly hadn't been there the last time Savannah had dropped in.

It would be stupid to call her. It would be insane. What would they even talk about? There was nothing Savannah could say to her.

Her legs quivered as she walked up the few steps to the huge front door of the multistory brownstone and rang the bell next to the correct name tag: *Dr. Loredana Valentini—Oncologist.*

# Chapter 2

ANNA APPROACHED BETHANY AS SOON as Mrs. McClary had left the salon. "What was that about earlier?"

"What do you mean?" Bethany asked, although she already had a pretty good idea what her colleague was referring to.

"You running after Miss Cortez."

"I didn't know that you knew her," Bethany said slowly.

"She's been here a few times. How do *you* know her?"

Bethany swallowed. "She's my ex. We've dated for five years."

"Oh." Anna grimaced. "I didn't know." She gave Bethany a compassionate look. "I'm really sorry. You must be... You must feel terrible."

"It's okay." Bethany shrugged.

Anna's whole frame stiffened. "I know it's often hard in relationships to deal with...well...such *things*," she mumbled. "Uh...how is she doing? Miss Cortez, I mean."

Bethany raised an eyebrow. She didn't understand why their breakup seemed to be such a big deal to her coworker. She frowned.

"Um. I don't know... She seems okay. She's in a relationship with someone else."

"Oh, I see." Anna ran a hand through her hair. She seemed worried she was on dangerous ground. "Well...if you see her, tell her she can come in anytime, and send her my best wishes."

Bethany's frown only deepened, but she nodded. "I will."

She grabbed a broom to clean up around the chair when the small glass door swung open and Amber came into the salon. She was carrying a huge tray covered with aluminium foil.

"Hey, baby." She balanced the tray on one arm and hugged her with the other. Then she kissed her on the cheek. "You done yet?"

With a bright smile, Bethany nodded, then rubbed Amber's back. "Almost. Just cleaning up. How are you?"

"Good. I brought us some canapés from work. Made sure to save you some of your favorite shrimp cocktails." She beamed at Bethany. "Thought we could take them to my place and pop in a movie?"

"Sounds good." Bethany nearly threw her scissors and combs back onto the shelf, then grabbed her jacket. "Bye, Anna. Have a great night."

As they left the salon, Amber wrapped her arm around Bethany's waist and leaned her head against her shoulder. "And how was your day? Anything special happen?"

Bethany thought back to Savannah. Then she looked at Amber, the woman she had grown to like, maybe even love, more and more in these past two months. Bethany really wasn't a friend of lying.

She sighed. "Actually…yes. I'll tell you over dinner, okay?"

Amber's eyes drew together, and she studied Beth's face.

"Okay," she said. "Tell me everything."

Savannah was so used to needles that she didn't even blink anymore when a particularly long one slowly disappeared inside her arm. She stared at the wall in front of her while Dr. Valentini took her blood sample.

She wasn't much older than Savannah, maybe only by a couple of years. "How are you feeling?" she asked.

"Like shit, honestly." She avoided meeting Loredana's gaze.

"I'm going to send these to the lab." Lory inched out the needle and put a cotton ball on the bleeding spot. "If everything's fine, we can start the next round very soon."

"I don't want another round of chemo," she said.

Loredana paused.

"What do you mean you don't want it? What are you talking about? It's not a matter of wanting, Savy. It's important."

Silence followed, punctuated finally by an ironic chuckle. "I'm done with it, Lory. Seriously." She grabbed her hair and tugged on it. The wig fell off in her hand. "You see this?" she said. "My hair's gotten longer again. It's almost covering my ears. I'm slowly getting back to my old self. I was at the hairdresser today, looking for a new wig, a slightly different one. But then I thought, what for, you know? It's pointless."

"Savy…" But Savannah waved her off.

"If I get a chance to feel normal again during my last days, then I want to take it. I don't want to go through all this shit again just so you can tell me that there are new metastases everywhere a few weeks later. It's a fucking joke. I'm so done with it."

Loredana closed her eyes and let out a deep breath.

"Savannah, where is this coming from? You're so mixed up today. I haven't seen you this way since…"

Savannah looked the other way.

"Are you talking to her again?" Loredana asked.

More silence. Loredana sighed again. "How? When? Where?"

Savannah toyed with her fingernails in her lap. "The salon. She's working there now."

"Did you tell her the truth?"

"No, I certainly did not tell her. And I'm not going to."

"You should," Loredana stated matter-of-factly. "You know you should."

"That's what you told me the last time." Savannah rolled her eyes.

"Yes, and I'll tell you over and over again. You should have listened to me back then. You've been feeling miserable. Before you broke up and after, not telling her didn't make anything better for you. Not at all."

"It wasn't supposed to make it better for *me*. It was supposed to make it better for *her*," Savannah half yelled, close to losing her temper.

Loredana shook her head. "Savannah, this logic, it's… Oh my, she's going to find out anyway sooner or later."

"Yes, when she reads about my death in the newspaper."

"Savy!"

"What?"

For a long moment, Loredana seemed at a loss for words. "Okay, so even if I don't want to contemplate it happening that way, let's talk hypothetically here," she finally said. "So she reads about your death. What then? Do you have any idea how that's going to make her feel? That you completely shut her off? She's going to think that you didn't trust her, that you'd rather deal with all of this alone instead of having her by your side."

"I wrote her a letter. She'll get it after I'm gone. It will explain everything," Savannah said.

"I think you're punishing yourself with this behavior, though I don't know for what reason. But then, why would you listen to me? I'm just your doctor, not your therapist or your confessor, right?"

"Right," she replied in a bitter voice.

"So? Are you going to meet her or what?"

Savannah nodded. "One last time…" she paused. "To say good-bye."

When Savannah arrived at their old favorite café downtown, Bethany was already sitting at a small table in the corner of the room. Her blonde, wavy hair hung in wide curls around her shoulders and shimmered in the dim light of the lamp above her. She stared at the table as she drew circles with her index finger on a napkin. She looked so innocent and beautiful, it broke Savannah's heart.

Bethany looked up, and their eyes met. She gave Savannah a warm smile, and Savannah returned it. They exchanged a brief hug when Savannah walked over. She sat down opposite her and folded her hands on the table, not sure what else to do with them.

"I haven't ordered yet because I wasn't sure you'd actually show up," Bethany said shyly.

"Can't blame you," Savannah mumbled.

They both ordered hot chocolates with marshmallows.

"So tell me," Bethany said after the waiter had left, "what have you been up to these past months?"

That question was one she'd expected. She pulled out her list of plausible stories.

"I've tried to change my life a little bit. Tried to live a little healthier, to see things, to travel." She tried to read Bethany's now-faltering smile. Her empty gaze carried a hint of sadness now.

This was awful. What on earth was she saying to her? It probably sounded to Bethany like *Oh, when you were gone, I started enjoying my life and travelling the world, doing all those things that I couldn't do with you.*

But what *should* she tell her? *I've been through chemo. Still, I've got metastases everywhere. Some days I've been too weak to leave the house, and the*

12

*meds make me throw up all of the time. I've tried to prepare myself for the fact that I'm gonna die. I've gone through hell. I've missed you every single fucking day.*

Yeah, that would be accurate. But not exactly helpful.

"I'm glad to hear you had a good time." Bethany sat up straight and pushed her shoulders back. She cocked her head at Savannah. "What places did you visit?"

*Doctor's offices. Hospitals. Therapists.* "I've been to Europe. Paris. Barcelona. Very pretty."

Bethany smiled again, wider this time. "I still want to see Paris. Is the Eiffel Tower really leaning to one side?"

"No, that's the one in Pisa," Savannah explained, but not in a snappish or lecturing way. In fact, it made Savannah smile. She would have loved to have seen all of those places with Bethany.

"Oh." Bethany blushed. "I always confuse France and Spain."

Savannah grinned. The tower was obviously in Italy, but she didn't feel like correcting Beth. Geography had never been her strongest suit. "Me too," she said instead.

"So, Loredana has been with you?"

*Damn.* Oh well. It had been nice for a moment to pretend that there had been no chemo, no CTs, no nervous breakdown. "Yeah, we visited her family in Italy. Beautiful landscape down there."

These lies were ridiculous. *Just change the subject.* "How did you meet your girlfriend? What was her name again?"

"Amber." Bethany smiled again. "I met her at the salon. But we haven't travelled anywhere, at least not yet. She's often at work. She has to cater events and stuff. She's an awesome cook; always brings home leftovers. It's nice."

"Sweet."

Bethany reached out over the table to capture her hand with her own. Savannah recognized it as one of Bethany's typical attempts to comfort her.

"I'm glad we are finally talking again," Bethany said. "I have to say, I was really sad that you cheated on me, but I'm not mad anymore. If this is what you needed to be happy, then I'm okay with that. I wasn't at first, but I am now." She emphasized her words with a nod. "You're special, Savannah, and I hated not having you in my life. We used to be so close, not only when we were dating but also all those years before that, you know? We were a team. Losing that really hurt me. I didn't feel complete."

Savannah nodded. She felt her hand get sweaty where Bethany touched it and felt the tears swell up again, tears she definitely could not let Bethany see.

"Remember when we were in high school? You always protected me. You've always been there for me, always made me feel safe. When I think back to all this, it still makes me smile, you know? We were best friends. Don't you think we can go back to that? I mean, not now, not right away, but…slowly? Maybe?"

Her voice sounded hopeful. Savannah almost sighed. Bethany was still that little girl she had always known, still the same Bethany whom she had fallen for a long, long time ago, the girl she'd always wanted to protect because she was just too trusting and gullible for her own good. She couldn't stand the thought that people would take advantage of that now that she was out of her life. She sure as hell hoped this Amber chick treated her well. She might be weak with disease, but she'd still kick that woman's ass if she had to.

"I don't know." She slid her hand from underneath Bethany's. "But I missed you too." She knew it was probably a bad idea to say this. It wouldn't help her get out of this situation, but it was a truth she couldn't deny.

"Would you like to see me again?" Bethany finally asked. "I mean, you could bring Lory. It could be like a double date. You'd meet Amber and I'll meet Lory, and we'll do something fun, like, I don't know, miniature golf? Sound fun?"

Now her eyes were practically glowing, and she clapped her hands together in excitement at the idea. Savannah cursed herself for ever having considered this could work out.

"Please, Savy. Say yes!" Bethany gave Savannah her best puppy-dog eyes.

She shouldn't have agreed to any of this. She shouldn't have walked into this café. Where would this stop? They couldn't become friends again. It wouldn't work. She wasn't even dating anyone, especially not her doctor.

"Just once," Bethany insisted. "If it gets too uncomfortable, we don't have to repeat it."

*Fuck this. I can't deal with this. I can't see her with another woman. I can't convince her I'm in a long-term relationship. This is a dead end. I can't agree to this. I won't. I will come up with an excuse now.*

"Savy?" Bethany asked carefully. She already looked a little sad again.

"Yeah…" Savannah closed her eyes. "Okay."

*Okay?* Savannah mentally threw her hands up in the air to tear at her fake hair. Even after all this time, she was still whipped. She couldn't believe herself.

"Awesome!" Bethany bit her fist, probably to tamp down that wide grin that threatened to overtake her face.

"Awesome." Savannah tried to sound at least a little cheerful for Bethany, who was emptying her cocoa and looking so happy and relieved, damn it.

Savannah dug into her bag to grab her cell and opened her text app. She shook her head as her fingers flashed over the screen to choose Loredana's name in her contact list and type a message:

*I need your help.*

# Chapter 3

"No way!" Loredana held her hands up in front of her body. "No way I'm going to pretend to be your girlfriend. Not only because I'm your doctor, Savy, but mainly because I will not encourage your lies. Nope."

"Lory, come on. I'm begging you here, okay? What am I supposed to do? Seriously, I need you to do this for me," Savannah said.

"I'll tell you what to do—you'll call Bethany and tell her that you changed your mind and that you want to talk to her, alone." Loredana looked Savannah straight in the eye. "And then you'll meet somewhere quiet, and you'll explain everything. And you'll see she understands and how you can finally be honest with her."

Savannah's teeth clenched. "I thought I could count on you." Her mind was already racing. People were obviously right when they said lying always got you into trouble, but it had worked out for so long, for over a year. She wasn't going to blow it all up now.

She flipped through the contact list on her phone. What was Plan B? She needed a female desperate enough to play her date—someone she could pay, someone Bethany didn't know. As she strode toward the door, Loredana's voice trailed behind her.

"Savannah, seriously, don't make this more complicated than it already is. And do me a favour and stop stressing yourself so much; you need to get some rest, I don't like seeing you so—"

The door slam cut off the rest. Already she was sending out texts to random ex-coworkers, but she and Bethany had been so close they basically knew all the same people.

The more she thought about it, the more she realized she was running straight into a dead end. This was a ridiculous plan. It was mean.

She had told many white (and not-so-white) lies in her life, mostly for her own benefit, but this was bad, even for her. What had started out as a plan to protect Bethany was transforming into a massive act that'd be impossible to keep going forever. She should simply cancel. Why couldn't she call her, tell her she was sorry, tell her that they should stop seeing each other? She had typed the text saying as much five times already and had deleted it each time. Five times she had tried to hit the damn *send* button, but she always backed out.

The truth was, after even a few minutes spent talking to Bethany, Savannah felt alive again for the first time in a year, but the feeling made her hands go clammy. Bethany reminded her of a time when her world was still perfect. When it was everything she ever could have hoped for.

But now, her life was falling to pieces, slowly slipping out of her hands. She had wanted to be the selfless lover who spared her girlfriend the pain of losing her. It had made total sense to her back then. But seeing Bethany had turned everything upside down again. How had she not anticipated the flood of feelings that would come back in that damn café? It had reversed all her selflessness into a cruel, selfish need to cling to Bethany, the person she still loved. She wanted to revel in the comfort of being near her when the whole of existence felt dark and senseless. Life was fucked up. She hated it.

Then again, what if fate really existed? What if it had been her goddamn fate to run into Bethany in that salon? Maybe somebody up there was telling her she was foolish for trying to get through this on her own?

No. Fate could go screw itself. It had made her sick in the first place. Fate was a bitch.

Savannah collapsed onto a bench in a nearby park and let herself rest a few minutes. A few children played hide and seek under the watchful eyes of their mothers. There was probably no way out of this, she thought. *Either tell Bethany the truth, or shut her out of your life once and for all.*

This fucking helpless feeling was eating away at her. Meeting Bethany's new girlfriend, getting Loredana to play her date—she had actually managed to tell herself that it was possible, that she could handle it, that it would go well. But now that date wasn't going to happen, and there was nothing to look forward to anymore. She'd have to go back to this emptiness, and the thought gutted her. She had been so used to it, so used to pretending she was okay without Bethany. Why had Bethany pushed for this? Why did she have to remind Savannah that she wasn't okay at all?

For the first time since their meeting, tears were running down her cheeks, hot and fast.

Her fingernails dug into her palm. Fuck her life, fuck Loredana, fuck Bethany, fuck her own body, its weakness. Even those stupid women watching over their kids pissed her off. Savannah decided she didn't care she had no right to feel this way; she certainly couldn't help it. In another reality, it could be Bethany and her over there in the play area. She would have made a kickass mother, strict but loving. And Bethany would have been an even better one. Hell, Bethany *was* going to be a great mother, only with someone else.

Her cheeks were completely wet by now, and she'd sort of forgotten that anyone else could see her. So she winced at the unexpected touch to her shoulder.

"Are you okay, sweetheart?" A tired-sounding, raspy voice interrupted her pity party. The old woman's hair was gray, and her wrinkled face twitched with concern. Savannah told herself that she would never look like that; she would never age. The sentiment sounded mean even in her own head, she thought.

"Can I help you somehow?" the woman asked.

Savannah jabbed at her tears to wipe them away. "No." She cleared her throat. "No thanks. Unless you're my fairy godmother and can grant me three wishes, I guess there's nothing you can do for me."

The old lady's expression widened with a beatific smile.

"You know, sometimes it seems as if everything's going wrong, honey, as if there'll never be a way out of our problems, but we should never give up. Even in the darkest times, there's still hope," she said. "And sometimes, when we least expect it, the happy times are waiting right around the corner."

Savannah sniffled, then blew her nose with a tissue the woman handed her. "It doesn't look like it." She started to sob. "It really doesn't look like it."

The woman sat down next to her and began toying with the golden amulet she wore around her neck. "Oh, honey, you're far too young and pretty to be so desperate."

An ironic laugh clutched at Savannah's throat.

"You know, sometimes," the woman continued, "when I feel a little sad or when I'm missing my husband, I try to remember what makes me happy. I try to live every day as if it were my last. That doesn't mean I have to do special things. I simply do what makes me feel better in that moment, go for a walk, have breakfast on my porch, call an old friend."

How she wanted to tell the woman to shut up, that she had no idea what she was talking about, but she could see the woman meant well, and Savannah didn't want to be rude.

"I'm sure you have a lot of good friends," the woman said. "Call one of them. Do you have a boyfriend? I'm sure such a pretty girl has all the boys waiting in line on her doorstep."

That got Savannah's eyes rolling. "You know, I'm really not in the mood to talk, actually," she decided. "I'm really sorry, but things are more complicated than you make them out to be. Not that I'd expect you to understand." She rose from the bench. "I should get going."

"I hope everything will be better soon. Try to appreciate the little things," the woman advised.

Savannah pulled out the closest thing to a smile that she could manage. "Will do," she said and continued her walk. She wanted to leave the park as fast as she could.

Her phone vibrated with a text just as she turned the corner. It was Maggie, her coworker from back when Savannah had still been able to work a real job. As she read the message, a jolt went through her, and her eyes widened. Her tongue ran over a sliver of her bottom lip as she read it once more to make sure she wasn't imagining things, but the words remained the same:

*Perfect, I really need the cash. Count me in.*

Bethany leaned back against Amber. She picked up some foam and blew bubbles through the bathroom. Amber was sitting behind her in the tub, massaging her shoulders and peppering soft kisses along her neck.

"How do you feel about the whole double-date thing? Honestly?" Her fingers caressed along Bethany's wet skin. "What do you know about Savannah's girlfriend, anyway?"

She sighed at Amber's touch and sank a little deeper into the tub as she attempted an honest answer. "I don't really know anything about her." The muscles in her jaw turned downward into a frown. "I know she's Italian and that she introduced Savy to her family in Europe. I suppose she's very pretty too."

"Don't you think it will be weird? I mean, she's the woman Savannah cheated with, after all. I don't mean to sound judgemental, Bethany. Like, I don't want you to think that this makes me uncomfortable or anything, because I'm fine with it. I just don't want you to get hurt by bad memories."

Bethany entwined their hands together and kissed Amber's fingertips. "I know. I've thought about it too. But she's been my best friend, you know? My best friend since I can remember. We've been inseparable since we were six years old. That's more important to me than the fact that our relationship didn't work out, you know?"

"I understand," Amber said slowly. Her chin rested on Bethany's shoulder. "And if it gets too weird, we can still leave, right?"

"Right." Bethany gave her girlfriend's hand a quick squeeze.

"Do you think she's changed? Savannah, I mean?"

Bethany had to think about that for a while. "Well, she seemed more… mature? I don't know."

"Was she immature when you knew her?"

"Um, sort of. It's weird, but there's something about the way she talks, the way she acts, that's more…serious. She used to be very outgoing when we were younger, always having the last word, always telling people what she thought of them, even if they didn't want to hear it. She was so energetic. She drew all the attention to herself when she entered the room. But I think she must have grown up a lot since then. When she enters the room now, she looks a lot…smaller."

Amber's fingers disentangled themselves. A beat of silence passed. "And how do you feel about that?"

It was hard to put into words what she had felt. It had been a different Savannah, though that didn't necessarily mean anything bad. Her hair had been different too.

"Beth, are you over her?" Amber asked so quickly that it was barely understandable. A moment later, she mumbled, "I'm sorry, I just…"

"Honey," Bethany whispered, "of course I'm over her. I mean, I love her, I do. But as I said, I love her as the person who's been so important to me my whole life, not as the person I want to date. She broke my trust, but I know she's a good person at heart, a good friend. But I want to be with you, okay?" she paused. "Just you."

She turned around to capture Amber's gaze with her own, then smiled and placed a kiss on her lips.

Amber smiled back. "Okay," she said. "I guess I just needed to hear that."

"All right, repeat it again!"

Maggie looked up at the ceiling with a loud huff.

"My name is Loredana Valentini. I'm from Orbetello, a pretty Italian city that's a one-hour drive from Rome. I have an older and a younger sister, and I'm a doctor. In my free time, I like to go jogging, and I play tennis—"

"What's your favorite movie?"

"Is it really that important?" Maggie's eyes scanned the long handwritten list of details she was supposed to remember.

"Am I paying you for this or not?" Savannah hissed back.

"Yes, geez, *chill*. My favorite movie is *Letters to Juliet*. My favorite singer is Tina Turner." She paused. "Do you seriously think anyone's gonna buy that I'm Italian? Have you looked at me? I'm a redhead, for God's sake."

Savannah responded with a glare that could cut diamonds. "You better make them believe it! And Italy has plenty of redheads, so I don't want any excuses."

Maggie frowned as she pushed the piece of paper aside and leaned over the table's surface, with her face close to Savannah's. "All this trouble because you don't want to tell your ex that you're sick? To protect her? What are you, some kind of nut? Isn't that all a little…*exaggerated*?"

It took all Savannah's willpower not to kick her out. She had never really liked Maggie, but she knew she had to at least try to play nice if she wanted this date to happen. Maggie was her last chance.

"Listen to me, Ginger. Stop your smartass remarks and play along, understand? I have my reasons, and I swear, if you screw this up, if you tell her anything, I'll kick your ass!"

"Okay, okay. So what exactly are we doing, anyway? Are we going out for dinner? Do I have to kiss you?"

Oh, good point. They'd have to seem intimate around each other, wouldn't they? The thought of being all touchy with Maggie was a total turnoff. "Look, we're gonna play miniature golf. Don't worry. We'll keep all the kissing and touching low level."

"Great."

"Great." Savannah forced out a smile and stood up. She pushed the list against Maggie's chest. "Have this memorized by tomorrow."

Savannah gave her a push toward the front door, glad when Maggie finally trundled out of the apartment with her study guide. Savannah's eyes closed, and she let out a deep breath. Back in the kitchen, she swallowed her medication and wondered how many wrong choices she had made in her life. If she was making herself go through so much trouble to be around Bethany again, why had she left her in the first place? Why had she wasted a whole year?

Her hands shook, and her breath was short when she pulled the blanket over her body in bed and stared at the ceiling, trying to sleep. This all made her head spin, and she felt lightheaded. But she needed sleep; she'd worry about the rest tomorrow.

Bethany and Amber were already waiting in front of the miniature golf course when Savannah and her "date" arrived in Maggie's rusty, old Geo Metro. Savannah's eyes widened at the sight of Bethany and Amber standing next to each other, and she truly hated the fact that Amber looked so damn flawless. The couple hadn't noticed them yet as they were still too busy giggling about whatever silly joke Bethany had just made.

Her motivation for this was slowly disappearing, yet Savannah had to get through this date. She had underestimated the effect it might have on her to see Bethany with someone else, and they hadn't even said hello to each other yet. She wanted her ex-girlfriend to be happy, but as long as Savannah was still alive, she was supposed to be *her* Bethany; she was not supposed to be with another woman who made her laugh and smile. This wasn't what Savannah had wanted to put herself through.

Bethany finally saw them. There was such a sparkle in her eyes as she waved them over. Savannah grabbed Maggie's hand, yanking her away from her attempts to kick the Metro's slightly deformed door closed. They walked over toward Bethany and her new girlfriend, hands entwined, and Savannah forced herself to smile, unsure whether to hug Bethany or go for a simple handshake.

Bethany made the decision for her by wrapping her arms around Savannah's thin body. The hug was longer than she had expected, and Savannah noticed her ex still wore the same perfume, a scent that engulfed her with memories. Their bathroom had smelled like this every morning when Savannah had entered it. Bethany was usually the first one showered, dressed, and preparing breakfast, while she had grumpily climbed out of the warm shelter of her bed.

When she finally let go of the embrace, Bethany turned to Maggie, her smile friendly but less warm than only seconds ago.

"Hi." She held out her hand. "You must be Loredana. Nice to meet you."

"Nice to meet you too," Maggie replied politely. "Savannah's told me all about you. Good to finally put a face to all the stories."

Savannah shifted from one foot to the other as she looked at Amber, who frowned at the scene in front of her. Savannah could almost see the wheels turning in the other woman's head, and she wondered if Amber was smarter than she had wanted to give her credit for. She hoped she was being paranoid, but part of her was sure that Amber would be able to put two and two together at some point. She was only dragged out of her thoughts when Bethany finally introduced Amber.

"Hi, Savannah," Amber said, in a bright yet distant tone. She bit her lip and took a few long seconds to extend her hand in greeting. "I've certainly heard a lot about you as well."

Savannah didn't miss the message there, and she couldn't deny that it made her angry. *Who do you think you are? Bethany's big protector?* She squeezed Amber's hand a little harder than necessary as she shook it.

"Sooo, let's get the clubs?" Maggie said, perhaps a little more loudly than necessary. They made their way over to the old lady sitting behind the counter. She handed them the clubs, a scorecard with a pen, and a little basket with four golf balls in different colors.

"Here, I guess you want the blue one?" Savannah handed Bethany the small blue ball.

Bethany plucked it from her hand and grinned. "Can I start?" she asked and was already storming over to the first mini-fairway, where they only had to play the ball around a corner to get it into the hole.

"Sure, babe. Start," Amber said and gave Beth a playful slap on her butt. Savannah gripped the club a little harder.

Bethany positioned herself in front of the tee and focused on the flag at the far end.

The other women waited patiently while Amber eyed Maggie closely with a sly side-glance. "I hope you don't mind me saying this, Loredana, but you don't really look Italian."

Savannah coughed.

"That's what I hear all the time," Maggie replied. "My grandfather was Scottish, you know?" She smiled. "Damn those recessive genes."

*Good girl*, Savannah thought to herself. They'd practiced that scenario often enough.

"Mm." Amber raised her eyebrows. "And what kind of doctor are you?" she continued.

Savannah stared at Maggie and could almost see her squinting with concentration. She had forgotten it, hadn't she? Great. Of course she couldn't rely on her to remember.

"Oh, one for the sick people," Maggie responded casually after a second. Bethany, who had repeatedly missed the hole, looked up from her ball and frowned. "Those are especially important," Maggie quickly added.

Savannah couldn't believe her ears. She cleared her throat before bursting into fake laughter. "Ha-ha. You're so funny, dear."

When Bethany's ball finally found its way into the first hole, Savannah quickly grabbed the red one out of its basket and started playing. They were slowly making their way through the nine different fairways, each one getting a little trickier. Bethany never managed once to sink her putt in less than ten tries, though everyone chose to ignore the rules at the sight of her sad, pouty face.

"I'm not the best putter."

As Bethany checked her scorecard, Savannah let her hand rest on her shoulder. "You're doing fine," she reassured her with a smile. "We all suck at this."

From the corner of her eye, she caught Amber's glare but chose to ignore it. She was highly aware that this contest wasn't about miniature golf anymore.

It was Savannah's turn again, and she could already feel the exhaustion kicking in. Miniature golf might not be the most active sport, but she wasn't used to being on her feet for so long. Constantly having to kneel down to grab the ball and using all her strength for the more forceful strokes was more exhausting than she'd expected. Cold sweat forming on her forehead, her vision was a little blurry, and her hands were beginning to shake in an effort to try and keep the club straight. She stumbled a step backward, right into Maggie, who managed to catch her.

"You okay?" she asked. Savannah nodded.

"I don't want to have to call the ambulance. You fainting was not part of the deal," she whispered into Savannah's ear.

Savannah pushed her away. "I'm fine," she hissed and tried to finish her game. She didn't dare look at Bethany, though she could feel her eyes burning holes into her back.

Savannah tried focusing on the red ball, but she could see two—no, three—of them, and it was hard to make out which was the real one. She tried to hit one but missed. Her breathing was getting shorter, and little black dots were dancing in front of her eyes. Heat wave after heat wave was rushing through her body, and she pushed down the need to rip off her suddenly terribly tight clothes.

*Just breathe.* She wouldn't allow herself to faint. Not in front of Bethany.

Her legs were shaking, and her head was spinning. The voices that surrounded her suddenly sounded so far away, as if there were cotton candy in her ears.

"I...I think I need to sit down for a moment," she managed to say and stumbled over to the nearest bench. Bethany dropped her club and was next to her in an instant.

"Savy, are you all right?" She patted Savannah's back.

"I...yeah... I guess I didn't drink enough water. You know how easily I dehydrate." It seemed like a plausible enough explanation.

"Hon, please get Savy some water and a candy bar, ok?" Bethany said. Amber looked skeptical but quickly made her way over to the little shop.

Maggie sat down at the other side of the bench, twirling her red locks around one finger.

"Don't get me wrong, but I think it's time to call it a day." She extended a strand of her hair and examined it idly.

Bethany didn't stop stroking Savannah's back until Amber arrived with water and chocolate.

She quickly unwrapped the Snickers bar and handed Savannah the water bottle.

"I thought you were a doctor. Shouldn't you help your girlfriend?" Amber asked Maggie, the judgment in her voice unmistakable. "One might think you'd know what to do in such situations."

Savannah was too weak to care that Maggie was useless in her role. All she wanted was to go home and lie down. *With Bethany next to me, stroking my back. And my hair. And maybe kissing my forehead.*

She shook her head. She had to get rid of these thoughts, these feelings. She softly pushed Bethany's hand away.

"It'd be nice if you could take me home now, Lory," she told Maggie, who shrugged and got up from the bench as she fumbled for the car keys in her pocket. When she finally found them, she held out her hand for Savannah to take and helped her off the bench.

Savannah turned and gave Bethany an apologetic look. "I'm sorry," she said. "But we were almost done anyway, right? And I didn't count the points, but I suppose you would have won."

"Of course she would." Maggie rolled her eyes. "It was nice meeting you both. Enjoy the rest of the day."

"Yeah," Bethany hesitated. "Feel better, Savy!"

Savannah knew she wasn't going to feel better anytime soon. In fact, she already felt worse. She closed her eyes for a second and tried to erase the image of Bethany's sad, concerned face. She sank down in the not-very-comfortable car seat and let her head rest against the window. What had she gotten herself into?

Her body had shown her once again that it was a bad idea to think she could hide behind this mask for much longer. What would Bethany think? Savannah had embarrassed herself. Should she call her when she got home and apologize for ending the date so abruptly? Maybe send a text? Do nothing?

She looked over to Maggie, who hummed along with the song that was playing on the radio. She had apparently decided not to talk. But Savannah needed to talk. She needed to fucking talk about this. She could call the real Loredana when she was home, but all she'd get would be a big "I told you so," something she didn't need to hear.

When they finally pulled up outside Savannah's apartment, Maggie cleared her throat.

"My money?" She held out her hand.

Savannah had to bite the inside of her cheek to keep herself from yelling at Maggie. She knew she had no right to be angry. Maggie had played her part as best she could and had done everything Savannah had asked her to. She owed her.

Still, she fumbled for the money and threw it on Maggie's lap. Then she got out of the car without another word and slammed the door shut, which took about all her remaining strength. Once inside her apartment, she made a beeline straight for her bedroom and let herself sink onto the mattress, not bothering to remove her clothes. Her hands were still shaking. She rolled over a bit and opened the drawer of her nightstand to get her medication. She swallowed it without blinking and added two sleeping pills. The knot in her throat was thickening, and tears built up in her eyes, but she hoped the drugs would kick in too fast for her to care.

Bethany still hadn't fallen asleep. She had been staring at the ceiling for hours now as if it'd soon present her with answers to all the questions in her head.

"Why are you torturing yourself?" Amber asked into the completely silent room.

"I'm not," Bethany said quietly.

"You are. It still hurts you. Even after all this time, it hurts, and I don't blame you, 'cause it's only natural. Plus, we both know that something is truly odd here."

Amber took Bethany's chin in her hand. Her green eyes held Bethany's gaze until Bethany let out a sigh.

"It's not odd. She's with someone else. These things happen. It's not—"

"That's not what I'm talking about, Beth," Amber interrupted her. "It's not weird that she's dating someone else; it's weird that she's *pretending* to be dating someone else."

Bethany tried to study Amber's face in the dark room. "I don't know what you're talking about," she mumbled and pushed Amber's hand away.

"Babe," Amber started again. "I don't know Savannah like you do, but she was really thin, Beth. Thin and pale and weak and shaky. Don't tell me she's always looked like this."

"She said she was dehydrated," Bethany replied.

"And 'Loredana'? I mean, seriously? The girl looked like Lindsay Lohan. I'm not buying it."

Bethany had never before seen her so emotional. "Amber, I don't know why you're getting angry. It's none of our business anyway."

"It became our business when you decided to go on dates with your ex again, Bethany!" Amber replied, her voice curt. "With your ex who cheated on you and lied to you and who's clearly still lying to you."

Bethany sat up in bed, turned on the lamp on her nightstand, and glared at Amber. "You've gotta be joking. These are all empty assumptions, Amber. This is making no sense. You're just criticizing because it bothers you that I'm seeing her again. At least have the guts to tell me the truth."

Her voice was higher than usual, louder than usual. Bethany paused. This was their first real fight, wasn't it?

"Are you closing your eyes to this on purpose?" Amber continued. "It's not that hard to see the obvious, Beth; it's happening right in front of your nose. You could save yourself a lot of pain if you'd be willing to see people for who they really are instead of always searching for the good in them."

"Are you calling me naive?" Bethany gripped the sheets a little harder.

"No, Beth. I'm worried, okay? Have you looked at Loredana's car?"

"I liked it. There was a rainbow sticker on the back door."

"Beth. It was an old Geo Metro, probably built like two decades ago. Loredana is supposed to be a doctor. Doctors have money. They can buy far better cars."

That was it. Bethany got out of the bed and put on her clothes.

"Where are you going?" Amber jerked upward. "It's the middle of the night!"

"I'm tired of people treating me like I'm some child," Bethany said, "as if I can't make my own decisions, as if I weren't a grownup just like everybody else, able to decide who to trust and who to talk to." The zipper to her bag closing sounded like a screech in the quiet of Amber's bedroom. "I'm tired of people telling me what's best for me. I can decide what's best for me, okay? And right now, that would be sleeping in my own bed."

When she got to the door, Bethany turned and winced at the hurt reaction in Amber's eyes. But Amber's words were making Bethany's head ache. She needed to get out of there immediately. The last thing she needed right now was Amber reminding her how deep the wound of her break with Savannah had been and how many unresolved emotions, fears and insecurities she was still carrying inside of her. "You're just jealous," she said with a groan. "You're making too much of all this because you're jealous that I used to be in a relationship with Savy." Even if she felt sorry for Amber, she knew she had to leave.

"Beth, if I'm making this all up, then why were you lying here, sleepless, staring at the ceiling all night?"

Amber's voice softened, and Bethany closed her eyes, as if that was what it took to make this all go away. They had been together long enough that Bethany could recognize the plea to stay buried in Amber's words, and she paused at the door, her fist clenching and unclenching around the handle to her bag.

"Don't want to talk about it," she grumbled finally.

Something in Amber's expression closed itself off, and Bethany bit her lip to see it. "Listen," she said, "I'll call you tomorrow, okay?"

Amber just nodded. "Beth?" she asked when Bethany was already almost out the door.

"Mm?"

"I love you."

Bethany froze. It felt good to hear Amber say it, to hear that she was loved. It did. But Amber was jealous, and Bethany couldn't deal with this when all she wanted to do was get some unhindered sleep.

But none of this was easy for either of them; she knew that. And what would happen if she left now? Could she really do that to Amber? And more importantly, did she really want to be alone right now?

She sighed, defeated, and sat down at the edge of the bed again.

Amber, meanwhile, looked confused, then spoke carefully: "Will you hand me my MacBook, please?"

Bethany nodded, handed Amber her laptop, and lay down next to her. She stared at the screen as Amber opened Google.

"What are you doing?" Beth whispered, but Amber didn't reply. Her eyes were fixed on the search bar where she typed in the name of the person who had confused them most during the night, *Loredana Valentini*.

"Two million two hundred sixty thousand hits?" she mumbled in frustration and tapped her chin. Her cursor went back to the search bar and Amber added the word *doctor*.

"Two thousand three hundred ninety two hits. That's something to work with," she said, scanning the page before finding the first link that looked promising.

"I fucking knew it," Amber mumbled and scrolled down the webpage she had just found. Bethany turned pale.

The woman who smiled at them from the screen was dark haired, had huge brown eyes and a friendly smile and was wearing a white doctor's lab coat. Same name. Same city. It had to be her.

"Believe me now?" Amber asked. "So, if this is Dr. Loredana Valentini, who was that girl we met today?"

Bethany had absolutely no answer to that. She didn't know what to believe anymore.

# Chapter 4

SAVANNAH HUGGED HER KNEES, WITH her chin rested on top. The blanket around her shoulders protected her from the fall breeze. The chill air brushed along the skin of her neck and sent goose bumps down her arms. She felt at peace in these moments, felt somehow connected to the beauty in this world. Not having to wear her wig in the mornings made her feel free.

There weren't many things left worth living for, but for Savannah, these quiet and beautiful moments were the rare exceptions. They made her want to do silly things, things she used to do when she was little, such as putting on her red rubber boots with the big white polka dots on them and running through the fallen leaves, jumping into puddles, and collecting chestnuts to take home. Those were happy memories—carefree. It would be nice to relive them, to feel the childish innocence of coming back home, exhausted from all the running and laughing, to her mom helping her out of her muddy clothes. Savannah would put on her most comfortable pyjamas and drink the hot chocolate her mom had made for her, always with extra marshmallows. The kitchen would smell of freshly baked muffins. It smelled like home.

The thought made her smile, and she wrapped the blanket closer around her.

Savannah didn't know if she was sad that she was going to die. Once she was gone, she'd simply disappear, and it would be okay. It was worse for the people left behind, much worse.

She had often tried to imagine how she would have felt if her and Bethany's situation had been reversed, how she'd deal with losing her girlfriend to some terrible disease. The idea alone was almost too awful to take, even though Savannah knew she was much stronger than Bethany. Bethany lived in a happy place. The world had always been beautiful in her eyes. Who was she to take that away from her?

She took a deep breath. The clear, fresh air filled her lungs, but she was scared. Why? Was she scared to die? Was she scared that it'd hurt? No. She wasn't scared of pain anymore; she'd experienced enough of that in the past months.

Maybe she was scared of leaving this world alone. Of course, she'd most likely have doctors with her, but they didn't count. She wouldn't have family, she wouldn't have a partner like Bethany. This was something she'd be facing all by herself.

She was tearing up.

She knew she could leave this world a little happier if Bethany's face—those blue eyes she trusted, those tiny freckles on her nose, that loving look so pure and full of honesty—was the last thing she saw. She knew it'd be easier to leave this world if she had Bethany's hand to hold.

But no. This was not going to happen. She needed to get herself together and face that. She was getting weaker every day, and as weird as it was to admit, she had given up. If another chemo could keep her alive for a few months longer, it wouldn't change a damn thing about her situation. She wasn't strong enough to do the things she enjoyed; she had lost the woman she loved. So why put herself through this miserable procedure again?

She had made her decision. She'd let her body decide when it was time to go, and until then, she'd try to enjoy these peaceful mornings on her balcony and the wind caressing her bare head—these beloved moments without her wig. These moments when she could just be herself.

She still had her memories, memories she could be thankful for, and those had to be enough.

Bethany sat up all night, brooding over the information Amber had dug up.

She was trying hard to find an explanation or indeed any reason to still trust Savannah, but she couldn't find one. She was left only with a burning need to know; she couldn't just ignore this.

She would have let it go if it hadn't been that this mysterious, confusing Loredana—this person who either had two existences or no existence at all, Bethany had no idea—had been the source of her breakup with Savannah.

There was nothing for it. Confronting Savannah was the only way she would ever get any answers. Bethany grabbed her coat and headed to the place she once called home.

It was hard to stand in front of her old front door after all this time. Why hadn't Savannah moved out? Wasn't this what couples usually did after a breakup, move into new places to rid themselves of the many memories still lying like grease marks in the old walls?

How could Savannah live her life with a new woman in these same rooms she had decorated with Bethany, in the same kitchen in which they had always cooked together? They probably had sex in the same bed she and Savannah had shared for years.

Maybe it had all been easier for Savannah. Maybe removing some pictures from the wall had been enough for her. Maybe this was none of her business, since Savannah had paid for most of the apartment by herself anyhow. Bethany's job as a hairdresser had never earned her that much money, and Savannah had always taken over the biggest part of the rent without complaint, without problem, without even a question.

She rang the bell with shaking hands. The times when she used to have a key to this door were long over.

She rang a second time, then a third, about to leave when she suddenly heard the crackle of the communications system.

"Who is it?" Savannah's weak voice asked through the speaker.

"It's me, Bethany."

Maybe this wasn't such a good idea. What would she do once Savannah let her in? *If* Savannah let her in. Would she confront her right away? Savy was most likely going to switch to her defensive mode once Bethany started asking her questions. Even if the real Loredana was not the person she had met the other day, she suddenly doubted that Savannah would just admit it like that.

There was a moment of silence before the static returned. "What are you doing here, Beth?"

Bethany bit her lower lip, deliberating her next words. "Can I come in?"

Silence again.

"Give me a minute, okay?"

Bethany rubbed her arms over her jacket as she waited. She stepped from one foot to the other. It was a cold day, a typical fall day, and she could see her own breath in front of her face when she talked. Three minutes felt like thirty, and she was relieved when she finally heard the buzzing sound of the door being unlocked.

She stepped inside and wiped her shoes on the old familiar doormat in the hallway. *Why change a doormat, right?*

The door to the apartment was left ajar. Savannah hadn't waited in the entrance to greet her.

Entering the room felt like an uncomfortable path down memory lane. It felt like coming back home from a long vacation, the moment when you step inside a familiar building and take in its particular smell, when everything looks the same yet feels different.

Savannah had changed some pieces of furniture and changed the pictures on the wall. But there was still the rug they had picked out together at IKEA back in the day. The same sofa was still there. Even the coffee stain she had once left on their armchair when Master Purr had jumped on her lap remained.

Poor old Master Purr. She missed him.

"I'm in the bathroom!"

Savannah's voice shook Bethany out of her memories. She tugged at her shirt and smoothed it down a few times before sitting down on the couch. She tried not to look around too much, to not take in too much more of that familiar feeling. She was only here to get answers, to clear things up. If Savannah had really lied to her for some weird reason, then she could get the truth and finally move on. She could accept that Savannah had a problem being honest with her. She'd leave Savannah alone and go back to her stable relationship. She'd apologize to Amber. Maybe she should have listened to her in the first place.

But then Savannah came out. Her old sweatpants were hanging loosely around her legs. Bethany knew those sweatpants; they were Savannah's favorites. Her Sunday pants, she'd liked to call them, although it was

Wednesday today. The white T-shirt seemed to be three sizes too large for her now. Her arms swam in the sleeves.

"Why didn't you call first?" Savannah asked. Her voice betrayed exhaustion and just a streak of confusion. She sank down on the armchair on the other side of the coffee table. "Oh, I'm sorry," she said. "I didn't offer you anything to drink."

"It's fine, I'm good," Bethany reassured her. *How on earth should I start this conversation?*

"I'm sorry I didn't call, it's just...I was in the neighborhood and..." She sighed. "Are you lying to me, Savannah?"

Now, that was a start. A very direct start.

Savannah's eyes widened at Bethany's words. Her face had already been pale; now it lost its last bit of color.

"Excuse me?"

"I'm sorry to come to you like this; it's probably stupid and probably nothing." Bethany cleared her throat. "Savannah, if you didn't want to see me anymore, you could just have told me, you know? I wouldn't be mad. I managed to get over you. I'm not planning to stalk you or whatever, so there's really no need to lie—"

"Why am I hearing the word 'lie' so often?" Savannah folded her arms across her chest. "Who said anything about lying? I don't even know what this is about!"

"It's just..." Bethany closed her eyes for a second before she grabbed her iPhone and opened the link to the real Loredana's webpage. She offered Savannah the phone.

"What the hell is this?" Savannah said. "All I see is some person who happens to have the same name as my girlfriend. Whatever you're trying to tell me, there are probably tons of people with the same name, I—"

"Please be honest with me." Bethany already felt tears well up in her eyes. She knew Savannah inside out. Savannah was lying. Oh, how she had wished to be wrong about this.

With a cold, even serious expression, Savannah put the phone back on the table and got up from her chair. "I guess it's for the best if you leave now."

"Why?"

"Because I'm asking you to. Because I didn't invite you. Because you can't just show up here like this and accuse me of shit. We're not together anymore. I'm trying to forget you!" There was more than hurt in Savannah's voice. She was angry. Hurt. Close to breaking.

Bethany stuffed the phone back into her jeans pocket and walked over to Savannah. She rested a hand on her shoulder.

"I didn't mean to upset you. I just wanted to say that if you feel like you can't be honest with me, if you feel like you don't want this and you need to hide things from me, then—"

Savannah narrowed her eyes. "You know nothing, Bethany! Nothing, okay? So shut up and stop trying to find answers that are impossible for you to find."

It was as if she had been slapped in the face. She stared at Savannah and hugged her bag tightly in front of her chest.

"What happened to you?" Bethany whispered, quickly brushing a tear away. "You used to be so honest. You once told me you always try to be honest with people, so why can't you be honest with me? Why can't you just tell me that you don't give a fuck about me and let me go?"

Savannah looked her straight in the eyes. Brittany thought she looked as if she were about to cry.

"Don't you think I've tried that?" she asked her, her voice shaky. "Do you think this is easy for me? Do you actually think I don't give a damn? Fuck it, Beth, you've always been the only fucking good thing in my life."

Bethany broke eye contact and looked at the floor. "Then why? I don't understand, please, I just... I don't understand." She didn't want to sound so vulnerable, so desperate.

Savannah sighed, looking defeated. "She's my doctor, Beth."

Bethany looked up, puzzled. She was beginning to get scared.

"She's my doctor, not my girlfriend. She never was."

"This makes no sense," Bethany said slowly.

"Bethany, I'm...I'm sick, okay?" Savannah's hand was shaking as she spoke, and she stepped away.

"Why sick? What's wrong? Do you have a flu? My mom knows about some great meds. I could—"

"It's no flu, Beth," Savannah answered, her voice softer again, as if part of her anger had evaporated. "The real Loredana is an oncologist."

Bethany's mind went blank. *Oncologist? What was that again? Damn it.*

"Onco...onco what?" she whispered, embarrassed.

"A doctor for cancer patients."

"I don't understand."

"I think you do."

*No. It can't be true. It's not.*

"How bad is it, Savannah? You're gonna be okay again, right? It's gonna be fine. *You're* gonna be fine. They can do a lot for cancer patients these days, can't they? Savannah, will you just answer me, please?"

"There's only so much the doctors can do, Beth. They have done their best, but—"

"Don't fucking finish that sentence!" Bethany suddenly yelled. She hated using swear words, but it was too damn hard to hold them back.

"Don't you dare finish that sentence and tell me that you're fucking dying, Savannah. Don't you dare tell me that you broke up with me, knowing you were going to die, to suffer all on your own. Don't say it, or I don't know what I'll do. I—"

Savannah stepped a little closer and put her index finger on Bethany's lips. "Shush."

She seemed to collect her strength. Then she finally managed to say what they both already knew.

"I'm dying, Beth."

The words felt like a knife in Bethany's chest. This had to be a cruel, fucking joke. She could have lived with a lot of things, but this? No. *Just no.*

"You're lying again. This is not funny," Bethany said, her voice numb.

"I'm not lying. For the first time in a long time, I am actually being honest with you."

She didn't try to hide the tears anymore that were now running down her cheeks.

"I'm dying because of liver cancer, and I've known for quite a while. And I wanted you to move on without me. I wanted you to live a happy life."

"You what?" Bethany growled. She felt her face turn red, felt heat flush through her veins and to her cheeks. "You're actually telling me that you broke up with me because you were dying? What kind of messed-up shit is this? No!" she cried. "Savannah, no! You cannot die. There have to be ways to make you okay again!"

"See?" Savannah said softly. "This is why I didn't tell you. This is what I wanted to avoid. I couldn't bear to have you go through this, to see that look on your face, to see you so scared. I didn't want this."

Bethany was crying bitterly now. She pushed Savannah's hand away when she tried to stroke her arm. "You fucking broke up with me because you didn't trust me to be there for you. You fucking broke up with me even though you still loved me and I loved you with all my heart. And you just pushed me away, made me feel guilty, and made me wonder what I'd done wrong. You made me wonder every single night what I did to deserve this, if I'd failed you. You break up with me and don't tell me you're fucking dying!"

She was yelling again. She didn't even recognize herself anymore. She knew she had never felt this way before. She had been sad and had felt crushed when Master Purr had died. She had felt desperate after her breakup with Savannah. But this? She hadn't thought she was capable of feeling this strongly, of feeling this terrible.

"I could have been there for you. I *would* have been fucking there for you. But you didn't even ask me! Didn't you think I had a right to know? We could have fucking been together, and you just stole away a year of my life with you. You're crazy, Savannah. You're fucking crazy!" She wasn't used to feeling so much rage nor being unable to control her own words.

Savannah looked down at the floor again.

"I'm sorry."

"How much longer do you have?" Bethany sobbed in a high-pitched voice, terrified to hear the answer.

"They can't really say. Maybe a couple more months. Maybe a year. I don't know."

Bethany felt her fingernails dig hard into her flesh. "Why did you do this to me?" she whispered. "Why?"

It wasn't a question that required an answer. There were no answers to any of this.

Savannah grabbed her hand and squeezed it tightly. "I never stopped loving you, Beth," she told her. It felt as if there were no oxygen left in the room.

Then, before Bethany knew it, Savannah's lips were on hers. She was pressing her softly against the wall.

They didn't move, not even their lips. They just stood there, pressed against each other, hearts thundering.

For only a moment, Savannah was with her again—her Savannah, her skin, her smell. They were so close. For only a second, it felt like home, as if it could all be okay, as if this were just a fucking nightmare. As if the whole past year had been just a stupid dream and when she opened her eyes, they'd be happy again. They'd be in their living room, about to cook dinner together, about to plan their future.

But she knew that once she opened her eyes again, reality would hit her once more. Savannah would still be sick. They'd still be broken up. Savannah would still die. And she was still dating Amber.

*Amber.*

Bethany woke up from her reverie and softly pushed Savannah away.

"I can't," she whispered, her whole body feeling hot. "I...I have to go."

Savannah didn't say anything, didn't try to hold her back. She just stood there as Bethany ran out the door.

Bethany ran along the streets, not even knowing where she was heading. She ran as fast as her feet would carry her until she felt completely exhausted and bent over to catch her breath. She could feel her pulse hammering in her temples, could feel her chest closing up.

She looked around and saw cars driving along the streets. People were talking to each other, chatting about the weather. Kids were on their bikes. Old couples and their dogs strolled on the sidewalks.

Life was still going on for everyone else. The whole city was entirely unaffected by what she had just found out. But for Bethany, everything had changed from one second to the next. A part of her felt as if she had died, and she had no fucking idea how to handle it. No idea at all.

# Chapter 5

As much as Bethany wanted to, she couldn't pick up the phone. She knew she owed Amber an explanation, and she wanted to tell her everything, but Bethany didn't feel as if she could talk about any of this yet. At least not with Amber. She couldn't put into words what she was feeling.

There was a feeling of betrayal because of Savannah's lies, yes, and sadness because of her illness. The terrible desperation because she couldn't do anything about it was killing her.

She knew she truly cared for Amber, but Savannah's confession, well, that changed everything. Bethany knew one thing for sure: she never would have broken up with Savannah. She had always been sure that Savannah was the person she loved most on this earth, and she would have been there for her through thick and thin. The fact that Savannah still loved her, that she had never stopped loving her, made everything entirely different.

Savannah was dying. The love of her life was dying. And she had lied to her about it.

There were no tears left; her eyes were dry, yet she couldn't stop sobbing. It was still hard to breathe, and her body shook until her chest hurt. Her throat ached too.

Whenever she managed to calm down, whenever she managed to empty her head a little, the thoughts kept coming back: awful thoughts about Savannah's funeral; awful thoughts of a world in which Savannah Cortez didn't exist anymore. Then it started all over again—the panic, the lack of oxygen, the need to throw up.

Part of her wanted to pack her bags, wanted to bang against Savannah's door and beg to be let back in. She wanted to hug her and never let her go, and snuggle up with her under the covers. They would just lie there and hold each other forever, until the very last day. They'd shut out the world completely and be around each other 24/7 to make up for the year they had stupidly lost. Bethany wanted to forgive Savannah for that, though it was a hard thing to do. A year had been taken away from her, a year she could have spent loving and supporting Savy through her illness.

Bethany did not go back. The bad thoughts kept controlling her mind, and all she wanted was to find a way to escape them, a way to get rid of a pain she had never experienced before in her life.

She had never been a fan of getting drunk to cope with her problems, had never used alcohol as a way to forget, but even Bethany had to admit that there was only so much a person could take in one day.

She wasn't used to drinking, so it didn't take her long to get to the state where the world started spinning. She had bought a bottle of tequila and sat down on a bench in a quiet area. She drank until she knew she couldn't take another sip without having to throw up.

Her face felt warm, her ears hot, and her vision blurry, but the pain remained. Why did people do this? Why did they drink when they felt bad? Bethany still felt bad, but now she also felt sick and dizzy.

Her hands were shaking, and she wanted to get away from this place, suddenly scared of being alone.

She knew she could call Amber. She knew she could take a cab home. But right now, there was only one person who could truly be there for her.

Bethany knocked at the door of the house she had grown up in. Her fingers were weak, and making a fist hurt. She tried knocking again, but the tequila made her feel as if her entire body were wrapped in cotton candy. Everything was happening in slow motion.

"Mom," she whispered. The sobs were shaking her body like hiccups, and the alcohol made it hard to see. "Mom! Mom, please open the door. It's me."

She could hear music from the inside, could hear her mother's singing voice.

Bethany grabbed her phone, ignored Amber's five missed calls, and dialled her mother's number with shaky fingers.

It took a while for the music in the house to stop playing and her mother to answer the phone.

"Sweetie!" she said. "How are you, darling?"

"Mom, I'm outside. Please let me in."

"Oh, how nice. Give me a sec."

The door swung open seconds later, and Bethany could see the smile on Eliza Peters's lips fade as soon as she looked at her.

"What on earth happened, baby? Oh my God, did Amber cheat on you? I swear I'll kick her skinny little ass. I might be almost fifty, but I'm still in good shape. I can take a—"

"You're fifty-three, Mom," Bethany slurred before the tears started running down her cheeks again.

"Details…" Eliza mumbled.

Bethany supported herself against the doorframe.

Eliza frowned. "You're drunk, aren't you?" She sighed. "C'mere."

Eliza dragged Bethany in for a hug, softly stroked her blonde hair, then kissed her forehead.

"What is it with you and your girlfriends? I don't understand it. Don't they see how amazing you are?"

"It's not that. She didn't cheat on me," Bethany mumbled, burying her face in Eliza's sweater. "In fact, neither did Savannah."

Eliza looked puzzled, softly pushing Bethany back to look at her face.

"What do you mean?"

"It's…it's Savannah. She's…"

More high-pitched sobs escaped Bethany, and she felt like a child again. Like a five-year-old girl who wanted her mother to tell her that everything would be okay, to come and fix her crushed little world. Except that no five-year-old ever got drunk on tequila.

"I should have figured. Shush. I should have known that no other person on this planet would cause my daughter so much heartbreak. Oh, sweet baby. You're still not over her, are you? I think it's time for jimjams and some food to sober you up."

Bethany nodded.

The phone was vibrating again, and Bethany drowned it with a pillow.

"Are you sure you don't want to pick up, honey? That's so unlike you. You know you have to tell Amber about this."

Being able to talk to her mother and hearing her advice had made the tight feeling in Bethany's stomach a little more bearable. Eliza had been there for her during the breakup from Savannah and had supported her during all her ups and downs—her mother's opinion mattered.

"I want to tell her, and I will. Of course I will. Right now it's hard, though, because I don't know what to say to her."

Her mom nodded. "You don't know if you still want to be with her now that you know Savannah still loves you."

Bethany raised her head.

"What? No! No, of course I want to be with her, I love her, Mom. I do."

"I know you do, honey," Eliza replied. "But people can love more than one person, you know? Your love for Savannah never disappeared. It's still inside you. All the old feelings are coming back, and it makes everything different. And it's mixed with the fact that Savannah is sick. I'd never blame you for being confused, sweetie."

Bethany was rubbing her temples now. She thought about popping some painkillers to get rid of the constant throbbing.

"Maybe you should tell Amber that you need a break, that you need to figure things out—"

"Mom! I know you loved Savy like your own daughter, but I can't just break up with Amber, I can't. It's not right. I want to be with her. She's always been good to me. And even if I can't deny that I still have feelings for Savy, she hurt me. It wasn't fair. It wasn't fair what she did to me."

The alcohol made her more emotional than she already was, and Bethany hated that drinking could have such an effect on her. Wasn't it supposed to make her forget, rather than feel twice as bad?

Eliza sighed. "You're right. But then you should really pick up your phone the next time Amber calls!"

"I will," Bethany agreed. Suddenly, she pushed Eliza's arm away and quickly got up from the couch.

"Where are you going?" Eliza asked.

"I think I have to puke." Bethany held her hand in front of her mouth, just in case.

"Honey, wait. I'll hold your hair!"

Savannah was still sitting in her living room, not able to move. She had spent the entire day staring at the wall. All she could think of was the expression on Bethany's face and the feeling of Bethany's lips against her own. She felt paralyzed.

The emotions, the fear she had seen on Bethany's features—they had been the main reason for this whole damn lie. She was sure she'd never be able to delete this from her memories.

Then again, how was she supposed to forget and to delete any memories at all? There wasn't enough time to forget before she'd be...well...gone.

She swallowed hard.

This wasn't worth it. This earth was a miserable place, a place in which she had taken away happiness from the one person who made everything a little better. She hated herself for it. She hated her body for doing these things to her, to them. She was destroying another person's life.

If she weren't such a big coward, she'd finish the job herself. She had thought of it many times. Had thought of ending things by her own will and not letting the disease win. She had always been her own fucking boss. What did this fucking cancer think—that she'd silently wait until it killed her? She might as well do it herself, do it her own way.

But then Loredana had kept reminding her that she wasn't a quitter. She was a fighter. She had been through enough shit in her life. If she wanted to show this damn cancer that it couldn't make any decisions about her life, then she had to fight. Fight with all the power she had left.

But what was even left to fight for now? Nothing. Fucking nothing.

It was time to leave this place.

No, she wasn't going to kill herself, not yet, but it was time to get away from here. Away from this apartment full of memories, away from her doctor who kept trying to talk her into another chemo, away from the woman she loved and whose life she was mixing up, away from everything.

She would jump into a plane and find a quiet place to die. She'd spend all her money in those last months and make it easier for everyone. It was time to say good-bye to Savannah Cortez.

Savannah got up from her seat and stumbled through the hallway. She hastily opened all of her drawers, searching for old photo albums, documents, certificates, or letters. Anything with her name on it. She carried it all outside onto her balcony and threw everything into the bin.

A swimming award from when she was six years old—bye-bye.

Pictures of herself smiling and standing next to her parents, adios.

Several certificates from cheerleading camp. Savannah hesitated. Her thoughts flashed back to the nights when Bethany had crawled into her bed in their dorm. They had been fourteen and far from dating officially.

*"I can't sleep, Savannah. I don't like cheer camp. The girls keep making fun of me, and it's exhausting. I mean, I love dancing but not if they drill me so much. The coach keeps yelling and yelling, and I just want to disappear."*

*"Hey, Beth-Beth." Savannah let her snuggle under her covers and wrapped an arm around her. "You're better than all of them, you know that, right? You're better than any of those other girls, and they are just being bitches because your talent scares them. And the coach—well, the next time she yells at you, just imagine she's wearing a big chicken costume. A really fat chicken with yellow feathers."*

The image had made Bethany giggle, and she had let her head rest on Savannah's shoulder. Sometimes they had kissed when they could be sure that no one was looking. At that point, she had been convinced that they were only curious. Little had she known that this girl would forever be her one and only, that she'd be all she could possibly want in her life.

Savannah made herself get rid of these thoughts. She stared at the certificates one last time before throwing them into the bin as well.

A few pictures—ones that reminded her of the happy days, of the careless times—were a little harder to throw away. She let her finger run along the images of herself, along her happy, smiling face. There weren't many of those pictures. A lot of them portrayed a young woman who was scared to show her true self, scared to deal with herself and her sexuality. The best pictures were those of her happiest years, living together with Bethany, finally having found herself, finally sure where she belonged.

Five happy years that she was thankful for. They should have taken more pictures in those years. They were the only ones worth remembering.

Savannah shook her head, close to crying again, so she threw the whole album into the bin before any particular picture might make her stomach turn around again. Then she grabbed her wig and stared at it.

*I don't need you anymore. This Savannah is long gone.*

She tried to ignore the lump in her throat when the wig ended up on top of the pile. She fumbled with the matches as she pulled them out of her pocket.

She stared into the flames of her past, watched the thick smoke being carried away into the sky.

Her gaze followed the red sparks flying around her, and she felt as if a heavy weight had fallen off her shoulders. She had the upper hand. She could make the decisions. It was up to her to decide when she was going to leave, and this was the first step. She needed this. She needed this to remind herself that she didn't want to look back anymore.

The heat radiating from the little fire felt warm on Savannah's skin, and she closed her eyes for a moment, listening to the rustling of the burning hair and paper in the bin. Tonight she was going to look for a place to travel to. For her final destination. She'd check her bank account and then make a decision. Beach? Mountains? Deserts? Forests?

Surely the Internet would provide her with a few ideas.

It was bright when Bethany opened her eyes again, and her heart skipped a beat when she realized she wasn't at home. She eventually realized she was still at her mother's place. Within seconds, her stomach tightened. The memories came back, her awful headache an instant reminder of the drinking, and the reason why she had done it in the first place.

It all felt like a bad dream, like her worst nightmare. But it wasn't a dream. It was real.

She needed to get out of this house. She felt dirty and sweaty and uncomfortable, and there were so many things going on in her head that she needed to sort out. She had to plan her next move, had to get a clear head and do something.

Bethany quickly stripped out of her pyjamas and put her jeans and shirt back on before heading down to the kitchen. Her mother was preparing breakfast, and the room smelled of fresh coffee.

"Mom, I have to go. I shouldn't have passed out like this. I'm sorry I was wasted. I—"

"Good morning, honey," Eliza greeted her and poured some orange juice into a glass. "Don't apologize. Sit down and eat something with me. You need energy."

"I'm sorry, but I can't."

Eliza sighed. "Of course you can, Beth. I understand that you're still mixed up and emotional, but there's nothing you can do that will change the situation right now. You might as well think of your health and give your body some vitamins."

Bethany didn't want to sit down. She grabbed the glass and drowned the orange juice in one. "I'll call you tomorrow, okay?"

"Beth?"

"Hm?"

"Please tell Savannah that I'm sending her all my best wishes, will you? And bring her over here whenever you want to. I'd be happy to have dinner with you two like in the good old days."

Bethany closed the top button of her warm coat and tried hard not to imagine Savannah and herself happily sitting at the dinner table with her family. She tried not to think of the many times Savannah had been angry with her because Bethany had started stroking her thigh under said table. Her hand had always travelled a little higher, and Savannah had nervously tried to push her away, her perfect-daughter-in-law-smile frozen on her face.

"Beth?"

"Yeah. Erm. I'll tell her that."

Sadness took over Bethany as she quickly hugged her mother and made her way over to the door.

"Bye, Mom."

Bethany felt terribly sorry for not having talked to Amber. She must be worried and angry. Seventeen missed calls, five texts.

The air outside felt much colder than a few days ago, and Bethany pulled her scarf a little tighter before dialling Amber's number.

"Bethany, where the *fuck* have you been?" Bethany had to hold the phone away from her ear. Sweet, calm Amber could obviously be loud and angry too.

"I'm so sorry, Ams. I was at my mom's."

"All night? Seriously, Bethany, I was this close to calling the police because you never answered my calls. Is there something you need to tell me? Seriously, tell me!"

"Ams." Bethany sat down on a huge stone to stretch her legs. She sighed. "Amber, Savannah is dying."

Silence.

"She's…what?"

"She has cancer, Ams. She only has a few more months to live. She lied to me to protect me. There's no other woman. There never was."

"Oh my God." Amber's voice didn't sound angry anymore. "Beth, I don't know what to say. I mean…how could she do that? Lie to you like that? Of course it's awful, and I'm terribly sorry to hear all this, but what are you going to do now?"

"Be there for her. That's what I'm doing."

There was no response.

"Amber, I *have* to. Oh my God, I've known her my whole life, and she's all alone. I can't let her be alone. I can't." *Damn these stupid tears. When will my tear stash ever be empty?*

Amber cleared her throat. "Yes, of course you need to be there for her. And I'm willing to help you if you need me. I'm really sorry. You must feel completely awful."

"It's been the worst night of my life," Bethany replied honestly. The air was fogging in front of her face. "And I don't know how to deal with it. Not at all."

"Why didn't you call me earlier, Beth? I'm your girlfriend, your partner. Why did you shut me out? Why didn't you contact me and ask me to be there for you?"

"I don't know. I was just completely confused."

It was the truth. Bethany had never been more confused in her life. And she had never been that drunk.

"I'm sorry," Amber continued. "I don't want to be too demanding. It's just… What is this going to mean for us?" Her voice sounded fragile now.

"Please, if you're going to break up with me, I need to know it right away. Please spare me an even bigger heartbreak."

Bethany felt a lump in her throat. She didn't want to lose Amber; she loved having her in her life. But right now, well, right now all she could think of was Savannah. All she could think about was how much time there might be left for her.

She tried hard to think rationally, tried hard to look at the situation from a more neutral perspective. Tried to see things the way she had seen them a week or a month ago when Amber had been the most important person in her life, and, no, she couldn't lose her.

"So? Are you? Breaking up with me?" Amber whispered, not able to hide the fear in her voice.

"No. I do love you, Ams. I want to be with you! You've always been so good to me. It's just…" Bethany tried to explain and bit her lower lip. "I need to be there for Savannah in these next months. If she lets me. Please understand that it has nothing to do with us or the fact that she's my ex. But she has no one. She's all alone. I don't want her to die alone. She needs me."

"I understand that," Amber told her sincerely. "I promise."

"Okay, um, thank you," Bethany replied, the phone still pressed closely to her ear.

"I love you," Amber said. Her voice filled with hope as she waited for Bethany's reply.

"I love you too. I promise to call you soon, okay?"

"Yeah," Amber said, and the call disconnected.

Bethany took a deep breath. The first step was done. Things with Amber were clear for now. She definitely had to talk to Savannah again.

It didn't take her long to get back to the apartment. When she got there, the front door was open. Their old neighbour, Mrs. McPherson, was cleaning the hallway, sweeping dirt out onto the pavement.

"Hi, Mrs. McPherson," Bethany greeted her.

"Bethany," she muttered. "Are you and Savannah back together?"

She sounded as if she feared the answer, and Bethany had to hold back a smile.

Bethany remembered the times she had run after Savannah to tickle her. They had almost always ended up physically fighting each other—in a playful way, of course. They had laughed and screamed and tackled each other until Mrs. McPherson had hammered against the wall with a broom. The next day, she had always given them both a very judging look and had mumbled something about young sex addicts and the terrible changes in society. Good old Mrs. McPherson. Bethany missed her.

"No," she replied and shook her head. "No, we're not back together. But we're friends."

"With benefits." The elderly woman had always had short, sharp things to say about Bethany and Savannah's sex life.

She focused back on her broom again, and Bethany pretended not to hear as she made her way to Savannah's apartment.

When she knocked, no one answered. She carefully pushed the door open. Savannah usually kept it open during the day and only locked up before she went to bed.

"Savy?" she asked and slowly stepped inside. "Savy, are you there?"

But then she saw her, and her heart skipped a beat. Savannah was asleep on the sofa, an empty bottle of wine on the floor and the laptop opened on the table. She was lying on her belly, one arm and one leg hanging off the couch, limp.

*Her hair. It's short.*

It took Bethany a minute to understand what was going on, and then the tears came back right away. Savannah looked beautiful. She looked thin and exhausted, but her face was as flawless as ever under her cap of short hair which barely covered her ears. Bethany noticed that it highlighted her beautiful features even more. Savannah was the prettiest woman she knew. And the short hair was a reminder of what she must have been through. Without her.

Bethany had heard stories about chemotherapy. Had heard about the side effects, about the weakness, the pain. And there was always the chance that it might not work.

Savannah had lost her hair. She had sat through countless hours of torture, and Bethany hadn't been there for her. Her chest closed up again, and her breath shortened. She had a silly need to stroke Savannah's head.

"Savy, hey." She tried waking her and softly touched her arm.

Savannah's eyes opened slowly, and she gave her a weak smile.

"Beth." For a moment, she seemed happy to see her, then her smile dropped away, as if she realized she wasn't dreaming. "Uh, Beth, what are you doing here?"

She batted at her hair and then frantically started searching around. "I—I got rid of my wig," she stuttered.

Bethany smiled. "You don't need it. You look beautiful."

Savannah gave her an incredulous look but didn't say anything. Bethany looked around the room and noticed that the walls were bare. Pictures were missing. It made her worry.

"Beth, I don't know why you're here again, but if it's about that kiss, I'm sorry. We—I mean…*I* shouldn't have. And I understand it was wrong, and it's definitely for the best if we don't see each other again."

"Why would you say that?" Bethany replied slowly, though it wasn't a question; it was more of an exhausted statement. Why would Savannah still push her away, even now, after everything was out in the open?

"Beth, I made my decision. It wasn't what I had planned. It wasn't what was supposed to happen. If you had never found out, you would have forgotten me at some point. But it didn't work like that. We ran into each other again, and it mixed everything up. But I'm leaving this time. I'm leaving for real, and it will make it easier, less complicated. And you can go back to your life and—"

"Shut up."

"Excuse me?" Savannah crossed her arms in front of her chest.

"You're going to sit down, and you're going to listen to me right now, Savannah." She adopted a tone that did not allow any protest. "I'm tired of all the plans that you've made. I'm seriously tired of it. Tired of the fact that you think you have the right to keep things from me and decide things over my head. I don't know what on earth made you do this, but trust me, I am still so, so mad at you."

"Beth—"

"I said listen to me. No interruptions!"

Savannah looked upset but kept quiet.

"I am still mad at you, and I can't believe you did this. I can't believe you would choose this life over me. Even if you say you did this to protect me, it's no excuse."

She took a deep breath and sat down in front of Savannah so their faces were on the same level. "You're still important to me, Savy. You'll always be important to me. I've loved you with all my heart, even long before we started dating. I grew up with you. You're a part of me. Don't you see that?"

Savannah tried to break eye contact, but Bethany softly grabbed her chin and made her look at her.

"You've made enough crazy plans for both of us. Now it's time that *I* make a plan, you hear me? It's my turn now. You owe me that much."

Savannah's chin quivered under Bethany's fingertips.

"I will not accept this decision you made, Savy. I will not let you leave this world alone. I want to be here for you. I always will. No matter what." She took Savannah's hand in hers and didn't let go. She looked into Savannah's eyes and kept her gaze strong. "I have a few demands."

Savannah stared at her with huge eyes.

"I demand that you let me do this," Bethany said. "I demand that you let me back into your life. As the girl who has been your best friend since first grade. As the girl who knows you better than anybody else in this world." She paused, then said, "I demand that you don't hide yourself from me. I demand that even if we're not together anymore, you will tell me how you feel, when you're scared."

Bethany squeezed Savannah's hand a little tighter when she saw a tear on her cheek. "And I want you to allow me to be scared too. I want us to be honest with each other. No more lies, never again. I want us to cry together when we feel the need to, I want us to hug each other when we need the comfort, and I want us to laugh together when we need to cheer each other up. I want you to take me to your doctor's appointments, I don't want you to go alone anymore. I want to know everything that's going on with you. I want to know everything about your medical condition. I'm going to read as much as I can about liver cancer until my brain feels like fried eggs, and then I want to talk to that doctor and hear everything she has to say about the situation.

"I can't accept any excuses, Savannah. I can't accept you leaving and not allowing me to appreciate every minute I have left with you."

Her cheeks were wet with tears, but her voice remained steady. "You're my best friend, Savy. You always will be."

Savannah brushed at her own tears with the back of her sleeve.

"Now you can say something," Bethany said.

Savannah's hands shook in Bethany's grip.

"Okay."

"Okay?" Bethany said. "That's it?"

"Yes. Okay." Savannah repeated, a small smile forming on her lips.

Bethany wrapped her arms around her frail body She held her close as if she'd never let her go again. She breathed in her scent once more, clinging onto her thin body. It felt like Savannah might disappear once she'd let go.

"You can't get rid of me that easily," Bethany mumbled into Savannah's hair. "And I won't let you leave me like this. Not like this, you hear me?"

"I hear you," Savannah said. "Loud and clear."

And it made Savannah laugh. For the first time in a long time, Bethany heard her laugh. Even if Bethany knew that the hardest months of their lives were still lying ahead of them—even if she knew the chances of Savannah's recovery were low, and the inevitable was going to happen—for this one moment, it felt as if everything was going to be okay.

# Chapter 6

"Um, ma'am? Excuse me, lady. You c-c-annot, erm, you c-cannot s-sleep here."

The thin lady carefully nudged Bethany with her foot.

"Ma'am, did you spend the night here?" she stuttered and shoved her thick glasses back on her nose with her index finger and said, "If you don't get up, I have to call my boss."

Bethany slowly opened her eyes and tried to remember where she was. She lay on the floor, her head between a pile of books and a thermos jug that had left a small coffee stain on the khaki-colored carpet.

"What time is it?" Bethany rubbed her eyes.

"It's quarter to eight, ma'am."

"Oh, okay, I suppose it's getting late," Bethany mumbled, yawning.

"Late, ma'am? Eight a.m., not p.m. You must have spent the night."

Bethany sat up and looked at her phone in panic.

"Holy shit," she whispered, quickly stuffing her things back into her bag. "I must have dozed off. I was tired. I'm really sorry." From the corner of her eye, Bethany saw the librarian checking out the books that had been lying next to her all over the floor.

One Renegade Cell: How Cancer Begins

Hope in the Face of Cancer: A Survival Guide for the Journey You Did Not Choose

Help me Live - 20 Things Every Cancer Patient Should Know

"I'm sorry," the librarian said as her gaze was fixed on the book titles. "I'm not going to tell my boss that you slept here. Just don't do it again."

*So that's how Savannah must feel most of the time. That's how people look at her when they find out that she's sick. They pity her. It's all in their eyes. No wonder she tried to hide it.*

Bethany felt dirty from having slept on the floor. Her back hurt and so did her eyes from all the reading. She had tried to get as much information on the topic as possible. Treatments. Coping methods. Everything. Bethany had been eager to learn, eager to get at least an impression of what was happening with Savannah. If she wanted to be part of her life, she needed to know how to help, how to give advice, how to take care of her. She wanted to know everything.

"Thank you." Bethany packed her bag. "I appreciate that."

"Good luck with everything," the librarian said.

Bethany stared, her mind blank for a second before she nodded. Luck. Yes. They needed a lot of that.

Bethany was almost half an hour late to work. She stumbled into the salon with her mascara still smeared across her face and her hair tousled.

"You're late," Patricia, her boss, hissed between clenched teeth. "Clients are waiting."

"I'm really sorry," Bethany blurted, out of breath from having to run to work. The stupid bus had closed its doors right before she had gotten the chance to hop inside and the grumpy driver had just taken off.

"It's a little chaotic at the moment," she tried to explain.

"Isn't it always chaotic in your world?" Patricia muttered, pouring some coffee into a cup she then pushed against Bethany's chest.

"Here. Drink that. And then use the restroom and clean yourself up. If you greet our clients looking like that, they'll turn around and run out the door."

Bethany did as she was told and took a closer look at her reflection in the mirror of the tiny bathroom. There were dark circles under her eyes, her skin looked flushed, and her hair was stringy. She really needed a shower.

Bethany quickly splashed some cold water into her face, then took a deep breath. *I just need to get used to this. It will all calm down eventually. Right?*

The situation with Savannah was still occupying her mind twenty-four hours a day. It had controlled her thoughts when she was at her mother's place, at Amber's place, at the library, and in her dreams. It was controlling her now.

Her first client of the day was Mrs. Robertson, a rather annoying person who talked a lot, and didn't pay attention to one word the client said to her. Something about her son, she assumed, as always. Bethany tried to finish the haircut as quickly as possible to get Mrs. Robertson to shut up, and she half-heartedly shortened the woman's hair. She was about to hold up the hand mirror so her client could take a look at the back of her head when she noticed she had messed up, big time. Part of Mrs. Robertson's hair was cut much too short, and the only way to fix it was to shorten it all at the neckline. Bethany's face lost its last bit of color.

"What is it? What are you staring at?" Mrs. Robertson asked, confused, her hand reaching out behind her head to examine Bethany's work.

"Oh my God, what did you do?" she shrieked. "Let me see!"

"I—I don't, uh…" Bethany stuttered as Patricia quickly made her way over.

"Out!" she ordered, her face hard. "I'm serious, Bethany. Get out and come back when you're your old self again."

Her hands shaking, Bethany nodded. She mumbled an apology before grabbing her bag and heading out. Her colleague Anna followed right behind her.

"Beth, wait a minute!"

Bethany sank down on a bench outside the salon. She bit the inside of her cheek to retain some control. *Come back when you're your old self?* How the fuck was that supposed to happen? When she was used to the fact that her best friend was dying? Or perhaps after her death? When Savannah was gone forever? Whoever got fucking used to that? When would there ever be a point when she didn't feel like crying, for God's sake?

Anna sat down next to her and gave her a concerned look. "B, what's going on? You wanna talk about it?"

"I messed up Mrs. Robertson's hair," Bethany whispered, her foot tapping nervously on the asphalt.

"Yeah, I got that part. But I mean in general. What happened?"

"Savannah happened."

"Savannah Cortez. Your ex," Anna said. Bethany nodded.

"You didn't know, did you?"

With a confused look, Bethany's chin shivered a little.

"The other day, when I asked you about her, you didn't know she was sick?"

Bethany shook her head.

"I'm so sorry," Anna told her and patted her thigh.

"I feel so embarrassed," Bethany admitted, not knowing what to focus her gaze on. She felt like hiding somewhere. Hiding forever.

"I only knew because she bought her first wig here. It was before you worked with us. She didn't talk much about it, she just... Well, it's awful. She's so young."

"Too young," Bethany agreed, hating the thick lump in her throat that didn't want to disappear lately.

"Are you gonna be all right?" Anna asked carefully, and Bethany smiled sadly.

"She won't be all right. That's all that matters at the moment. And it sucks."

Anna nodded, then gave Bethany a hug. Bethany appreciated it. She appreciated that Anna stopped asking questions, because it was clear that there was nothing more to say. She appreciated being close to people, appreciated the chance to let herself go and close her eyes and be embraced.

"Do you want me to call Amber?" Anna offered. Bethany shook her head.

"I'm good. Thank you, though."

"I'll talk to Patricia, okay? Don't worry. Plus, let's be honest. You did Mrs. Robertson a favor. Ladies her age should stop trying to look like teenagers. Shorter hair will be much better for her."

Bethany smiled as Anna gave her one last, brief hug and went back to the salon.

Bethany reminded Amber of a sad and lost little puppy. She had left her own work as early as possible in order to pick Bethany up and take her home. She had heard how upset Bethany was over the phone and had not wanted to waste another minute.

If Amber were honest with herself, part of her felt as if she needed to prove to Bethany that she could rely on her. That she herself should be the first person Bethany would call in an emergency or whenever she needed help. That she was the one person who should first pop into Bethany's head whenever she needed to talk.

But now, with Savannah being back in her life, in *their* life, Amber was scared.

Scared of losing her girlfriend, scared of all the emotions that were slowly bubbling to the surface. She had never seen Bethany like that before. Bethany was changing entirely, and it terrified Amber.

"Beth, I'm sorry about what happened," she began, holding the door of her car open for Bethany to get in. "I think you should take a few days off. To clear your head."

Bethany buckled up, looking out of the window. "Yeah, I thought about it. I might really need some time off."

With a smile, Amber started the engine.

"That's good. You should really try to recover. It was a lot to take in. I don't know, we could maybe get away for a few days, if you like? I'm sure I could arrange something at work. Maybe go on a weekend trip? We've never done that. It would be our first little vacation."

Bethany stared at Amber as if she were from another planet.

"You're kidding, right?"

Amber cleared her throat, focusing on the road.

"Why would I be kidding?" she asked slowly and gripped the wheel a little tighter. She had a pretty good idea where this was going, and she certainly didn't like it.

"Ams, I'm not going to leave town when my friend is dying," Bethany said as if Amber were out of her mind.

Heat rushed to Amber's face. She could feel her pulse race as the jealousy and insecurity kicked in. "Beth, you are my girlfriend. All I asked you was if you wanted to get away with me for a weekend to clear your head, because you obviously don't feel good. I was thinking of *you* and *your* health."

Bethany remained quiet.

"And what's with the silent treatment now?" Amber asked. "Okay, if you want to spend the time with Savannah, then just say so."

"Don't even start an argument about this, Ams, or you can stop the car right now. I am not going to fight about this. She needs me, and you said you'd be okay with it. You said you wanted to help me, but how is it helpful if you're trying to take me away from here and make me forget? It wouldn't work anyway."

Yeah, it wasn't going to work; Amber was sure of that by now. Nobody had a chance against the ex, right? Wasn't this some unwritten law or something? That you could never compete with someone's first love? Oh God, what was she even thinking? They were talking about a sick person, and she should show more compassion. This was the wrong place for jealousy.

Plus, Bethany was the most kind and caring person Amber ever knew. She was doing the right thing. Who was she to try and hold her back?

"I'm sorry," Amber offered slowly, glancing over to Bethany, who still wasn't looking at her. "What do you want to do now? Want me to take you home?"

Bethany nodded. "Actually, I want to take a hot shower, get cleaned up, and then head over to Savy's. There are still a few things I need to discuss with her, and, yeah, she needs some real food, some proper groceries."

Now it was Amber's turn to remain quiet.

"I don't know," Bethany continued. "I think we need to get used to each other again, but once Savannah feels a little better and more open toward me, you could come with me sometime. You could get to know her a little better."

Amber raised an eyebrow, not sure what to say about all this.

"I don't want you to think that I'm shutting you out of my life," Bethany said. "I want you to be a part of this. I need you to be."

And Amber wanted to be part of it too; she really did. But it was going to be hard for all three of them. The situation was a dead end, and Amber wasn't sure what her place in all this could be.

Bethany was biting her nails. Amber reached over and gently placed Bethany's hand away from her lips and down onto her lap, where she held it. She loved Bethany. She knew it with all her heart. Bethany was worth fighting for. Amber was not going to let her slip away. She would not repeat the mistake Savannah had.

"You sit down on the couch and watch some Sweet Valley High!" Bethany ordered when Savannah opened her door. She looked at her in surprise. "I'll cook."

Bethany was carrying two huge bags of groceries, so full that Savannah was worried she might drop them.

"Let me help you."

When it looked as if Bethany would object, Savannah frowned. "Don't give me that look. I can carry some groceries."

She needed Bethany in her life, but she didn't need her to do everything for her from now on. She was still her own person. She still had her pride.

"What are you cooking?" Savannah asked, and Bethany smiled as she put some fresh vegetables on the counter.

"You'll see. Relax and let me do my thing."

"Okay, okay," Savannah raised her hands in defense. "Tell me if you need any help."

"Will do." Bethany smiled and opened the book she had brought with her. It was full of colorful Post-its with little notes that bookmarked the best recipes.

Bethany started slicing the vegetables, and Savannah found watching her much more interesting than what was happening on TV. It was a good feeling to see her there. To see her moving around the kitchen, opening all the drawers, knowing exactly where the knives and bowls and pans were kept. It was as if she belonged there. It used to be their kitchen after all. It felt as if nothing had changed, even though everything had.

After a while, the whole apartment was filled with a delicious smell, and for the first time in a long time, Savannah found herself to be truly hungry. In the past months, eating had mostly been an annoying necessity for her, something she did to keep her strength up, but nothing she truly enjoyed. Now she could feel her mouth water, could feel some true anticipation inside of her belly. She looked forward to sitting down with Bethany at their dinner table and seeing her smile while they ate.

Savannah sipped the last of her tea and pulled the sleeves of her sweater over her hands when she felt a cool breeze blowing in from the open window. She loved being inside when it was cold outside and that it was already getting dark in the afternoon. She loved the warm feeling of soft wool on her skin and hot tea in her belly. And that Bethany was here with her. It felt like home again. It felt right.

Bethany had started setting the table, forks on the right and knives on the left because Savannah was a leftie, while humming a song to herself.

Savannah gave her a warm smile.

"It looks great," she said in awe as she looked at the casserole bubbling in the oven. "And it smells even better."

"A few more minutes," Bethany stated and smiled back at her. "I hope you're hungry."

"Yeah, actually I am," Savannah said. Her gaze landed on the book that was lying on the counter. She felt the knot around her stomach tighten.

The Cancer-Fighting Kitchen: Nourishing, Big-Flavor Recipes for Cancer Treatment and Recovery.

Bethany made her way over to her.

"What is this?" Savannah asked slowly, running her finger over the cover of the book.

"I did some research," Bethany admitted. "Are you mad?"

The question was barely more than a whisper, and Savannah felt that all-too-familiar little pain in her chest. Mad? No. No, she wasn't mad. Oh, she was angry at the fact that what had seemed so normal and familiar was now overshadowed by depressing reality again, but was she mad that Bethany was doing everything she could do to keep her healthy?

"I'm not," she said softly. She looked over her shoulder to give Bethany a small, reassuring smile.

"It's just… Why are you doing this?"

"I want to know as much as I can, Savannah," Bethany explained. "I want to be prepared. I want to be involved."

Her voice was serious now. Savannah knew she was trying to make her point very clear.

"I told you before: You are important to me, and I wasn't lying. I want you to take good care of yourself and do the best you can. I want you to eat healthfully and…"

"And what?" Savannah asked.

"And I want you to let me come to your doctor with you tomorrow."

Savannah swallowed. "How did you know?"

Bethany stepped from one foot to the other. "I kind of saw your calendar, that little notebook. It was lying open in the kitchen. I'm sorry."

"Don't apologize," Savannah said with a sigh. It's okay. I...I guess I want you there with me."

They smiled at each other for a long moment until Bethany finally pointed at the oven. "We should eat before the food burns. I put too much effort into this to screw it up at the finish line."

"I'm gonna burst!" Savannah moaned. She leaned back in her chair and was rubbing her belly. "This was a food orgasm."

"I'm glad you liked it," Bethany giggled.

"Seriously, where did you learn how to cook so well?"

Bethany went quiet for a moment, the smile frozen on her lips.

"Uh... Amber taught me a bit. She knows a lot of tricks that made cooking easier for me. You remember she works at that catering service, right?"

"I remember," Savannah answered, not looking entirely happy with that information. Savannah looked tired, more tired than usual. She was a little pale.

"Are you okay?" Bethany asked carefully and Savannah nodded.

"I'm okay, I just... I think I need some rest soon. If that's okay with you."

"Are you kidding? Of course it's okay. Energy is important."

Savannah shuffled over to the sofa and lay down.

Bethany carried dishes to the kitchen sink and ran hot water over them.

"Savy?" Bethany asked, her voice shy.

"Mm?"

"I just wanted to say that I'm happy you're not wearing that wig anymore."

Savannah avoided her gaze.

"I'm still getting used to being without it." She sighed. "My hair used to be one of my best features."

Bethany shook her head and laughed. "Your hair was always perfect, and it still is. I'm just glad you're letting some of your walls down again. I feel like I can finally see the real you after all this time."

Savannah gave Bethany a sad smile. "I just wish I felt more confident again. I wish I wasn't so terrified of showing you how...how *weak* I've become."

"Weak? Are you kidding me?" Bethany said. "You are the opposite of weak. Savannah, please allow yourself a break every now and then. There's no need to keep up any facade in front of me. You can always be honest. I've seen you in all kinds of situations, remember? Hell, you've seen *me* in all kinds of situations. You don't have to feel awkward or insecure in front of me." Bethany knelt before the couch and squeezed Savannah's hand.

"Remember how I felt when I got chicken pox? I was twenty or twenty-one, and I was so whiny and embarrassed because I thought chicken pox was only for children. Do you remember that?"

Savannah smiled at the memory. "I do, Beth. How could I forget?" she whispered.

That provoked a laugh. "It was itching so badly, and I was crying actual tears. I thought I looked so ugly with those spots everywhere, as if I had had pimples all over my body."

"It wasn't that bad," Savannah replied with a grin.

"Oh, it was, and you know it! But you never made me feel bad about it. You insisted on helping me with the lotion, and you told me you loved me and that there was absolutely nothing to be embarrassed about. You always knew how to make me feel better. You even let me choose the movie we watched that night, and we both know that's never a good idea."

Savannah chuckled. "Oh God, you made me watch *Dude, Where's my Car?* for the umpteenth time. It's such a fucking awful movie!"

"We should watch it again sometime," Bethany teased, and Savannah rolled her eyes.

"Oh, oh, or remember that one time when I called you at work?" Bethany blurted out, barely able to control her laughter.

"Oh God, Beth," Savannah groaned and buried her face in her own hands.

"Why are you reminding me of this? I had put you on speaker in a meeting because I thought it was important, and what did you do? You told me you were naked and thinking of me. That was even more embarrassing for me than it was for you, and now it's supposed to make me feel better?" Savannah asked, frowning.

She had wanted to kill her assistant that day. And she had wanted to kill Bethany.

"C'mon Savy, I can see that hidden smile on your face." Bethany stuck out her tongue. "We totally got over it, and in fact," she mumbled, "I think we had the best sex ever when you came home."

Bethany bit her lower lip and batted her eyelashes in a manner that Savannah had always loved. Oh sweet, innocent Bethany, who had never been that innocent after all.

"Yeah, it was pretty good," Savannah admitted, nodding and smiling to herself at the inevitable wave of memories.

This had been only a few weeks before Savannah had gotten her test results. A few weeks before they had told her about the liver cancer. Before she got the news that it had already spread and it looked bad for her. Before her world had fallen apart and she had slowly started pushing Bethany away. It was a happy memory. A careless one.

Bethany's hand was still lying on Savannah's, but their smiles had faded. They were looking at each other in a way that didn't require words. There was trust between them. A deep kind of trust that they had started building up years ago. Sure, there had been lies, sure there had been betrayal, but in the end, this strong connection remained.

Their faces were dangerously close to each other when Bethany ran her hand through Savannah's short hair. There was absolutely nothing weak about the picture in front of her. Savannah was a beautiful, strong woman. Absolutely stunning.

"You're so pretty," Bethany whispered. "Still so beautiful."

Savannah blushed and closed her eyes for a moment to take in the feel of Bethany's soft strokes.

"I'm glad you're here," she whispered, but before Bethany had the chance to answer, her phone vibrated in her pocket. They were drawn back to reality in an instant.

"Ams? Yeah. Yes, I'm still here. No. Well, if you like you can pick me up here, sure, yes. Okay. Then I'll see you soon." Bethany cleared her throat.

"I promised to come home to her tonight. I wasn't there last night, so I guess I have to, you know? I don't want her to be—"

"Beth!" Savannah interrupted her. "Beth, it's okay. It's totally fine. I want you to enjoy the rest of the night. I'm no fun anymore. I'm really fucking tired."

"But I'll see you tomorrow, right? I can pick you up. Around ten a.m.?"

"Sounds like a plan," Savannah replied before pulling Bethany in for a tight hug. Sometimes Savannah was scared, deep down, that it might be the last time they'd see each other.

Bethany put a small kiss on Savannah's hair and rubbed her hands along her back.

"Sleep well, okay?" she whispered and Savannah nodded.

"You too, Beth. And thank you for…er…the food."

Bethany smiled. The food. Yeah.

# Chapter 7

"How was it?" Amber asked.

Beth had no response.

"Beth?"

"Uh. Yeah, sorry." She stirred herself and began to change into her old sweats before sinking down onto the bed. She hadn't said a word since Amber had picked her up from Savannah's place, and she still didn't feel like talking.

"We ate together."

Amber swallowed visibly. "You cooked?"

"Mm."

Amber sighed and changed into more comfortable clothes herself. Bethany thought that it must be pretty obvious that she didn't want to talk, so she headed to the bathroom to brush her teeth and wash off her makeup. She looked at herself in the mirror and took a deep breath. This wasn't easy. Was there a guidebook that told you how to deal with such a situation? How to rebuild your relationship with your dying ex while still having a romantic relationship with another woman? If so, she really needed it.

"You want to watch a movie or something?" Amber asked.

Bethany shrugged.

"Or, like…maybe talk?" Amber pressed.

Bethany patted the spot next to her on the bed.

"I just feel drained, to be honest," Bethany said. She wrapped an arm around Amber, who rested her head on Bethany's shoulder.

"You were on my mind all day," Amber whispered, snuggling closer to kiss Bethany's cheek and neck. She found the spot at Bethany's earlobe that always made her giggle when she nibbled on the skin there, but Bethany didn't react. Amber let her hand travel upward and lifted Bethany's shirt in the process.

Bethany's thoughts went wild. It wasn't wrong to want to be close to her, was it? They hadn't had sex in over a week, and she missed feeling her, missed kissing her. Shouldn't it be nice to let go a little? To enjoy being cared for? Still, Bethany's body stiffened under Amber's touch, and she could do nothing but stare at the ceiling. She couldn't enjoy it. Damn it.

"You okay?"

"Sure," Bethany mumbled and turned her head to look at Amber. The smile on her lips was sad. Bethany reached for Amber's hand and kissed her fingertips.

"Do you need space?" Amber asked.

Bethany sighed and closed her eyes for a moment. She thought about her response, even though she knew that being alone must be an awful feeling for Amber. Bethany never thought long about what she said; usually she just said what she wanted to say, blurted out whatever was going on in her mind. It was a quality that she knew Amber had always appreciated.

"No. I'm glad you're here. I don't want to be alone."

Amber nodded again and moved closer to finally capture Bethany's lips with her own. "I love you," she whispered against her lips, and Bethany allowed her to deepen the kiss as she slowly opened her mouth. Amber let out a soft moan. Her right hand was running through Bethany's soft, blonde hair while her left hand moved further under Bethany's shirt and lightly stroked her breasts.

She parted Bethany's legs with her knee and moved fully on top of her, not once breaking their kiss.

Bethany let her, her own hands slowly stroking up and down Amber's back, her fingertips leaving featherlight strokes.

As Amber's thumb continued to encircle Bethany's nipple, her mouth travelled to Bethany's neck. Kissing. Biting a little. Her knee was still positioned between Bethany's legs, and she pressed it down a little more firmly.

Bethany barely reacted.

"Hey, you with me?" Amber asked. She took Bethany's chin in her hand to make them look at each other.

"Yes. Yes, keep going," Bethany encouraged her. She closed her eyes and focused on the pressure against her clit and the hand that was slowly making its way between their bodies and tugging on her sweatpants.

Amber let her hand wander into Bethany's panties. Her fingers travelled further down when she froze, one finger resting at Bethany's most intimate spot.

"Wow."

"Wow, what?" Bethany asked confused.

Amber crawled off Bethany's body and lay down next to her, staring at the wall.

"Why did you stop?"

"It's okay, Beth. I guess it's not the right time. Obviously."

Bethany didn't say anything, and only one look at Amber told her that she probably felt stupid or angry.

She could feel her hands getting sweaty, could feel her heart beating a little faster. What was she supposed to do? It was an emotional overload for her, and all of her thoughts and feelings were occupied elsewhere, but she didn't want to push Amber away. She had tried, hadn't she? Didn't that count for something? It all sucked. It truly fucking sucked.

Minutes passed, and the silence was suffocating as Bethany felt her own fingernails dig into the palms of her hand and she heard Amber sob.

"You would rather be with her, wouldn't you? You're mad at me for picking you up earlier. You wanted to stay but felt guilty, so you came with me. Am I right? I stand no fucking chance against her. You still love her. Just say it."

Bethany closed her eyes and started massaging her temples. "Please."

"Please, what?" Amber blurted out, her voice close to breaking.

"Please don't. Please don't make this harder for me than it already is."

There were so many things left unspoken, so many things she knew Amber wanted to say to her, things she could read in Amber's eyes, which were rapidly moving from left to right as if they were searching for a way out of this mess. But no words came out.

"Let's just sleep," Amber whispered and dragged the blanket all the way up to her chin.

"I'm going to go with her to her doctor's appointment tomorrow morning," Bethany whispered back. The statement came out sounding so strident in the otherwise dark and quiet room.

"Yeah. Of course you are."

It was the last thing they said to each other that night.

When Bethany woke up, Amber had already left. It was unusually early for her, and Bethany knew she didn't have to cater any event before the late afternoon. A look at her phone told her she had to hurry up a little, so there was no time to worry about any of this right now. She would try to fix things later.

On her way over to Savannah's, a tight knot rested in her stomach, a nervousness she wasn't used to. Talking to her doctor would make things more real, wouldn't it? Hearing them talk, worrying about test results. It was an awful feeling, being so powerless and having to rely on what some person in a white coat was going to say about her best friend's future. She had never imagined being in such a situation. Life had been so carefree for her for so many years.

Bethany picked up some bagels for Savannah on the way, though she herself wasn't hungry. She knew she couldn't take one bite without feeling as if she were going to throw up.

When she arrived at Savannah's house, Savannah was already waiting for her outside. She was wearing her warm black coat and a fluffy scarf around her neck. Her makeup and her entire outfit looked perfect. Savannah would never leave the house in a simple jeans or a sweater. As sick as she might be, her outward appearance would always remain flawless.

"I hope you didn't wait too long," Bethany said as Savannah got into her car and buckled her seatbelt.

"Not more than two minutes," Savannah replied and greeted Bethany with a hug.

"You nervous?" Bethany asked her, though she knew Savannah probably wasn't any more nervous than she was herself.

"Whatever they have to say, I'm just happy you're there with me." Savannah smiled and let her hand rest on top of Bethany's.

Bethany didn't know where she was going, so Savannah told her the directions to the doctor's office while keeping the mood casual with random small talk.

She nibbled at the cream cheese bagel Bethany had brought for her, even though Bethany could tell that she didn't have an appetite either. Some silly part inside of her wished they were going on a nice trip right now. To the zoo, shopping, ice skating—anything but this. They'd turn up the volume of the radio, and Savannah would sing to one of her favorite songs. Bethany missed hearing her beautiful voice. She wondered if Savannah were ever going to sing for her again.

They'd have a bag with snacks on the back seat. Happy sandwiches with smiley faces in pink Tupperware. Savannah had always insisted they'd buy something on the way, but Bethany was a fan of lunch boxes. In the end, Savannah would always give in and prepare the sandwiches while Bethany filled a thermos with hot chocolate. Then, later, when Bethany opened the lunch box, a funny face would greet her—bread with cucumber eyes and a carrot nose. Savannah might have been tough as hell, but she was also the cutest and most loving person Bethany had ever met.

But, they weren't going on any nice trip.

"There it is." Savannah pointed at the big brown building with many windows behind a huge parking lot.

Walking up the steps to the entrance door felt like going in slow motion, as if Bethany's body were trying to resist entering the building. They took the elevator for several floors and walked along a bright corridor to a plain office door. Bethany saw the name plate next to the door, saw the word *oncologist*, and the past days were quickly replaying in front of her eyes. How had they ended up here? After seeing Savannah at the hair salon, everything had happened so fast.

Savannah stepped inside before her, and Bethany spotted the small dark-haired woman who got up from her chair to greet them. So this was the real Loredana, the woman whom she had heard so much about, even if they were mostly lies.

"You must be Bethany," the small Italian woman greeted her with a handshake. "Uh, I mean, Miss Peters."

"Bethany is fine," she told her, smiling. "Or Betty Boop; that's what they used to call me back in high school," she added, trying to lighten the mood. "You know that cartoon, right? She's sexy, loves to dance, she—"

"Beth!" Savannah whispered between gritted teeth.

"Sorry," Bethany mumbled. "I don't know what I'm saying sometimes."

Loredana laughed and motioned both of them to sit down on the other side of her desk.

"How are you feeling today?" she asked Savannah, and Bethany could see her eyes automatically scanning Savy's body. She tried to read her mind, tried to make out the tone in her voice, but she could do nothing but wait.

"I'm okay, I think," Savannah replied, toying with her sleeves. "Still tired pretty often."

"What about pain?" Loredana asked, and Bethany felt her head turn hot. She hadn't thought much about the side effects. The fact that Savannah was sick had been a lot to take in, so the idea of her best friend suffering from actual tumour pain was something her mind had avoided.

Savannah swallowed. She quickly glanced at Bethany before facing the doctor again.

"My back hurts a lot when I move too much—also my arms. The occasional cramps have gotten worse, I guess. But all in all, it's okay. I'm taking my medication."

Bethany grabbed Savannah's hand under the table and squeezed it hard. Her own hand was icy cold, as if all the blood in her body had flooded to her head to make her cheeks turn red. She could feel her own heartbeat pounding throughout her body.

"Yeah, that's why I'm asking. If it gets worse, I'll prescribe you some stronger pain meds."

"I'm good."

Loredana's smile faded as she looked at Savannah again, her gaze suddenly serious. "Savy, I've looked at your results, and you don't have to pretend for anyone, okay? The meds can make it better, I promise. I can add some pills for muscle relaxation. It will help with the cramps."

It was Savannah's turn to squeeze Bethany's hand now, and Bethany could feel her shift nervously on the chair next to her.

"I said I'm good."

"Okay."

Loredana was staring at some papers in front of her now and took some notes. "I want to talk to you about the test results, Savannah. Would you like us to do that privately?"

"No," Savannah said, her voice firm. "I have nothing to hide from her."

"All right."

Bethany wanted to ask questions, wanted to hear Loredana say that it was going to be okay, but she remained quiet. She didn't let go of Savannah's hand and had no idea what to focus her eyes on. She had to be strong for Savy. She had to.

"Savannah," Loredana started, her eyes still fixed on the papers, "I'm afraid it turned out that the last chemo didn't quite take effect as much as I had hoped. There are several more metastases on your spine, so it's not surprising you feel pain in your back."

Bethany bit the inside of her cheek hard, Loredana's words echoing in her mind.

"Also your lungs are affected and—"

Savannah raised her hand, motioning Loredana to stop. "It's okay. Lory, it's all right. I didn't want that chemo anyway. You know that."

"What are you talking about?" Bethany blurted out and immediately let go of Savannah's hand. "What do you mean you didn't want it? What does this all mean? I read so much about cancer, so much about liver cancer. The books said it could be healed. They said that—"

"Bethany," Loredana interrupted, her voice soft. "The thing is that liver cancer is extremely hard to detect in the beginning. The symptoms are usually small, mostly not noticeable enough for a patient to get worried and consult a doctor. In most cases, such as Savannah's, liver cancer is detected during a routine examination, at a point when it's already too late to treat it before it gets the chance to spread. Do you understand that?"

Bethany nodded, her cheeks flushed, her eyes tearing up.

"We were all hoping that the chemo would be more effective, but the cancer is very aggressive. Of course, it would be possible to try another round, but I have to admit that I don't think it is going to increase Savannah's life expectancy. If anything, it is going to make her feel a lot weaker."

Tears were streaming down Bethany's cheeks now, and Savannah tried to smile as she patted her leg under the table.

"Hey Beth-Beth," she said softly. "No tears; it's not a surprise."

Bethany felt like pushing the goddamn chair away and running out of the small, suffocating office. She pinched her skin hard, wanting to wake up from this nightmare. She would wake up, right? It was just a fucking nightmare.

Of course, Savannah had already told her the most terrifying facts. Of course, she had told her how slim her chances of recovery were. But hearing all this out of a doctor's mouth? Too real. Too fucking real.

"We are all here for Savannah's support, Bethany." Loredana tried to calm her down. "We have the most excellent doctors here at our local hospital. You're not alone in this."

"Excuse me," Bethany breathed out, feeling her breath shorten, the lack of oxygen making her dizzy. "I... No. Can't. Need air. I'm sorry."

With that, she stood and stumbled to the door. She pushed against it, frustrated when it didn't open. Her vision was blurry, but she could still make out the *pull* sign and finally managed to open it and run into the hallway. She started coughing and quickly unbuttoned the first few buttons of her blouse, scared of suffocating or fainting. She made it to the closest window and ripped it open to breathe in some fresh fall air.

She didn't know how long she had been standing there, her mind empty and dark, until a warm hand touched her on her back.

"Beth," Savannah whispered, her thumb brushing along her shoulder blade.

"I'm so sorry," Bethany said, on the verge of sobbing. "I just couldn't hear it. I wanted to be here for you, and now I messed it up completely. Oh God."

"No, no, don't say that," Savannah's chin rested on Bethany's shoulder. "I'm the one who's sorry. I should have known what she had to tell me. I never should have brought you here."

Bethany turned to look Savannah straight in the eyes. She was so brave. Savannah was so fucking brave. And she herself was weak, a coward who was trying to be strong for her but felt so close to breaking.

"It's not your fault you're sick."

"It's not your fault either, Beth. It's no one's fault. It's life. And life often sucks."

She wondered how Savannah managed not to cry. How wasn't she terrified? How did she do it? She took Savannah's hand again, which felt warm against her cold one—and stared down at their entangled fingers.

"I can't even begin to imagine a life without you, Savannah. I don't want it. I don't want it."

Here she was, feeling like a little child again. She let herself sink onto the floor, back pressed against the wall behind her, and Savannah sat down next to her to wrap her arm around her shaking body. The floor was hard and cold, but Bethany didn't care. She buried her head in Savannah's neck and let her tears soak her shirt. She was going to sit here forever. She didn't think she'd ever be able to get up again. She'd just drown in this moment in Savannah's embrace.

*She* was the one who should be comforting *her*, not the other way around. Savannah should be crying, and Bethany should be the one telling her she'd always be here for her, should be the one kissing her hair and whispering comforting words into her ear. But she didn't have the power. How did Savannah manage to make her feel so safe in a situation like this? She had always been the strong one, always held Beth close, always protected her. She had been her rock, her whole life long.

Bethany clung to the fabric of Savannah's jacket as if her life depended on it. She wanted this feeling to go away, yet she didn't want this moment to end. Because every other moment would bring her closer to the day Savannah would die, right? Couldn't they find a way to stop time? To stop all the clocks on this planet?

"Shush," Savannah whispered, pressing Bethany closer so she could feel Savannah's heartbeat, could feel it hammering in her chest, so close to her own. She wished it would never stop beating. It felt like the most important sound on earth.

"You know, Beth," Savannah started, her voice barely audible. "I thought I was going to be okay with, you know, dying." She twirled some blonde locks around her finger and put a small kiss on Bethany's hair. "But now, with you back in my life..." her gaze dropped.

Bethany snuggled up closer to her on the dirty floor of a public hallway.

"With you back in my life, I kinda don't wanna go now."

Bethany chose not to say anything. She knew exactly what it meant. There was no turning back. Savannah still loved her the same way as she had always loved her. And she felt it too. Stronger than ever before.

Bethany wanted nothing more than to spend every free minute with Savannah, but she had clients waiting for her at the hair salon and hadn't yet gotten the chance to tell Patricia that she was going to take some time off. However, she was going to do that today. No doubt about it. Now that she knew Savannah's prognosis, she wouldn't be able to go to work every day as if nothing had happened. She wanted to do everything she could to be there for Savannah.

They were still sitting in the car in front of Savannah's apartment, not quite willing to say good-bye yet.

"We can do this, right?" Bethany still felt weak from all the crying earlier. "I told you we'd get through this together, and I mean it. I promise I won't break down like that again."

"You don't have to promise me anything, Beth," Savannah replied. "And I understand if you say you can't do it. I—"

"Stop. Don't even say it."

"Okay." Savannah started chuckling after a while, looking down at her lap.

"What's so funny?" Bethany asked, confused, wondering what on earth would be worth laughing about right now.

"Nothing. It's just that it's kind of silly, isn't it? The dreams you have as a kid or as a teenager? The things you never do because you think you have all the time in the world to do them?"

Bethany nodded slowly, still not getting the joke.

"Did you know that for a while, when I was younger, I had this pretty ridiculous dream of owning a motorcycle and driving off into the sunset with you? I pictured you in a sexy leather jacket, how you'd sit behind me, and we'd look all kick-ass, like a real power couple. I thought that one day we'd go on some super-awesome Route 66 journey, hang out in biker bars, make out in cheap motels on the way."

She laughed, and Bethany felt her eyebrows raise. Yet, she knew there was also a small smile tugging on her lips at this quite absurd image.

"And now look at me! I can't even play miniature golf without almost passing out. Pathetic."

"Don't think that," Bethany told her. "There are plenty of things you still *can* do. And we'll do all of them."

"Well, I'll certainly never own a motorcycle," Savannah added with a wink.

For a second, Bethany wanted to tell her they could still make out in cheap motels, but she quickly remembered that they weren't together anymore. It was so weird, being around Savannah. She had been part of her life for so long that it sometimes felt as if nothing had changed. But there was someone else in her life now. Someone she truly cared for. Bethany felt guilty for even having these thoughts.

"I guess I should head to work now," Bethany said slowly, looking apologetic.

"I know." Savannah smiled. "Thanks for coming with me today, though. I truly appreciate it. A lot."

Bethany smiled and leaned in to hug Savannah. Another one of those extremely long hugs, Bethany thought. Another hug that said, "I'm scared to let go."

"We'll talk later?"

"We will."

Bethany waited in the car until Savannah had disappeared inside. She stared at the door for a few moments longer after it had shut and thought about the things Savannah had told her. She thought about her dreams, about how much time they might have left together, when suddenly an idea crossed her mind.

It was never too late to make dreams come true, was it?

Savannah had spent the rest of the day in front of the television, trying to distract herself. Part of her was still guilty for making Bethany go through all of this, especially since it was exactly what she had tried to avoid by not telling her about her illness. But now that everything was out in the open, the thought of having her back in her life meant more than anything. Even if she'd never kiss her again, even if they could never be lovers again, Savannah was willing to take what she could get.

The ringing phone startled her for a second. She didn't recognize the number on the display. It couldn't be Bethany, and it couldn't be Lory. Both of them were the only people who had lately called on her cell.

"Hello?" she asked into the speaker, half expecting it to be someone who had dialled the wrong number.

"Savannah?"

"Yes?"

"This, uh, this is Amber."

Savannah felt her body stiffen. What did she want from her?

"Everything okay with Bethany?" she asked, worried, immediately scared Beth had gotten into a car accident on her way to work. It would make sense, considering how emotionally mixed-up she had been all day.

A sigh at the other end. "Yes, everything's okay."

"Thank God. But…what do you want?"

There were rustling sounds at the other end, and Savannah wondered what the hell this call was about. "Hello?"

"Yeah. Yes, sorry. I shouldn't have called, it's just…" Savannah heard her swallow. "I'm just gonna say it. Is anything going on between you two?"

"Excuse me?" Savannah asked. She couldn't be serious, could she? A jealous phone call?

"If so, please tell me. Gosh, I'll back off, okay? I'll leave her, as much as it'll hurt me. But I can't be in this relationship, thinking something's going on behind my back. I can't."

"You cannot be serious," Savannah told her, offended. "Hate to break it to you, Amber, but I'm sick, not a home-wrecker."

Silence.

"I'm really sorry. I'm just kind of desperate, and I'm sorry about what you're going through, but Bethany is not the same around me anymore."

What could she say? She was already wondering if she should tell Bethany about this more-than-inappropriate phone call. Of course Bethany would be different after going through this illness with her. What did Amber expect? It didn't make Beth a cheater.

"Listen to me, girl. I don't know you, and I don't know much about your relationship with Bethany, but what I *can* see is that you're obviously having trust issues. Your girlfriend has been my best friend my whole damn life, and her being there for me just shows what a fucking amazing person she is. She's also the most honest person on this planet. I don't even see how you can doubt her for one second!" Savannah yelled into her speaker, not remembering the last time she had been this upset.

"But you're still in love with her, aren't you?"

The accusation overwhelmed her. Still in love with her? Fuck, she couldn't even let her thoughts go that way. She couldn't allow herself to consider these feelings, because it would only break her heart. Of course she loved her. Of course she wasn't enjoying any of this. Of course part of her constantly felt like kissing Bethany when she was around her, but she had other things to worry about. She had to worry about death—if she let herself imagine that Bethany was sleeping with another woman every night, she'd go crazy. She blocked these thoughts and feelings out with everything she had.

"I can't believe you're even going there," Savannah said slowly, her voice cold as ice. "This is crazy."

"Yeah. Yeah, okay. Shit, I'm sorry. Fuck."

Savannah had to shake her head. She could hear the embarrassment in Amber's voice, but that didn't make things better.

"I'll hang up now," Savannah said, not waiting for Amber's reply.

Damn, this was a fucking mood killer.

Savannah lay down on the couch again and stared at the television that was still running in the background. What did this person want from her? That she back off? That she tell Bethany to stay away? She couldn't do it. She couldn't do it anymore. It was too late for that. It'd kill her faster than this fucking cancer would.

Sometimes she wished she hadn't stopped talking to all of her other friends, that she hadn't relied on Bethany as much. What had happened to the people she'd been friends with during high school? What about Joan Foster? What about Cobie Mills? Why had they all stopped talking at some point? When had she shut everyone out?

She hadn't even talked to her own parents in ages. They had never gotten along very well, and after their divorce and that huge fight, all three of them had gone their separate ways. Was it time to call them? Shouldn't they know their daughter was dying? Would they even give a shit?

Ugh, she shouldn't have picked up the phone. All she could think of now was that Bethany was dating someone else and that this person didn't even appreciate her, didn't trust her. Because, seriously, there was no reason to be suspicious, was there? Bethany didn't love her like that anymore. Right?

Savannah sighed, then undressed to take a hot bath. Her upper stomach hurt, and she felt like closing her eyes for a bit and enjoying some warm water on her skin.

Before getting into the tub, Savannah looked at herself in the mirror. Huge brown eyes were searching for anything desirable in her reflection, but they found nothing. Short hair, thin arms, bony hips, and her skin a shade of yellow. Savannah shook her head before turning away from the image. There wasn't much left of the old pretty, confident Savannah Cortez, the cheerleader who had dated the beautiful blonde girl in her cheerleading squad. The beautiful blonde was now dating another beautiful blonde, someone worthy of her beauty.

Savannah stepped inside the tub while the water was still running. She loved the sound of running water more than anything else. It was the most comforting sound on earth, and there was no better feeling than closing your eyes, listening to the water, and slowly feeling the tub fill around you, surrounding you with its warmth. For maybe an hour, she'd be able to shut out the world and not care about anything or anyone.

Savannah shut off the water. It didn't take long for her to fall into a dreamless sleep.

When she opened her eyes again, the water around her had turned cold. She groaned. Her back hurt from having lain in the tub for longer than she had planned. She carefully climbed out and wrapped herself in a huge orange towel. A look outside the window told her it was dark, and she figured she was tired enough to continue her nap in her actual bed.

After having dried off most of her body and hair, Savannah put on her pyjamas and headed back to the living room to take a look at her phone, which was still lying on the table. Hm. No message. No call.

Savannah couldn't help but feel a little disappointed, having hoped to hear something from Bethany before she went to bed. It had probably all been a bit too much for her, and she most likely needed some time to herself to process the events of the day.

She made her way over to the kitchen and heated up some water to make herself a cup of the green tea that Bethany had brought her yesterday. Apparently some professor in Europe had healed his cancer by drinking one glass every night before sleep. Savannah didn't believe in such things, but the tea came from Bethany, which was reason enough to drink it.

Just as she put a bit of honey into her cup, Savannah winced at the sound of the doorbell. What the hell?

She wondered if it was Bethany after all, coming by to tell her good night in person, and she felt a wave of excitement in her belly. She rushed over to the mirror to see if she looked completely awful, only to realize that she did.

"You should call me first," she muttered to herself and quickly brushed her hair as she let the door buzz open.

She peeked outside to see if it really was Bethany and not some random stranger she had let in, but what she saw made her catch her breath.

"What on… Are you… Oh my God, are you serious?"

From one second to the next, Savannah had forgotten about her wet, tousled hair and her blue pyjamas. Bethany was walking up the stairs to her apartment, grinning.

Bethany's blonde hair was curly, voluminously falling over her shoulders. She was wearing tight, baby-blue jeans, dark cowboy boots, and a black leather jacket with a little brown fox tail hanging out of one pocket. Dark makeup was highlighting her eyes, and she was carrying a box wrapped in colorful paper.

"Gonna let me in?" She smiled. Savannah nodded in awe, slowly stepping away from the entrance.

"Please don't tell me you're here with a motorcycle, Beth, 'cause I'm pretty sure neither you nor I know how to ride such a thing."

Bethany chuckled. "Don't be silly, Savy. Here, open it."

Savannah shook her head, not believing what Beth was doing but enjoying it nonetheless.

She carefully unwrapped the box and opened it, laughing as she found another leather jacket in it.

"Should be your size. Try it on."

Savannah did as she was told. The dark leather jacket felt a little too large around her waist but definitely fulfilled its purpose.

"Look what's in your pocket!" Bethany ordered cheerfully, and Savannah put her right hand into her jacket to find something that felt like a little plastic toy. She pulled it out and grinned as she examined the little red thing.

"My very own motorcycle." She laughed, but there was a small tear in her eye that she didn't want to let Beth see. This was too cute for words. This was why she loved Bethany so much.

"You like it?" Bethany asked her.

"Love it, Beth."

"Awesome!"

With that, Bethany hopped next to Savannah on the couch and wrapped her arm around her as she held a Polaroid camera in front of their faces.

"Hold up the motorcycle and smile!" she ordered.

"Beth, I look like crap."

"Shush, do it!"

Savannah had to roll her eyes, but it made her laugh nonetheless right when Bethany pressed the shutter button and the flash light blinded their eyes for a second.

Bethany took the Polaroid out of the camera and shook it until the image appeared.

"There's something else in the box," Bethany told her.

There was indeed something else lying at the bottom of the package—something that looked like a book.

"What is it?" she asked Bethany as she let her thumb run over the green cover.

"Look inside."

She carefully opened the cover and was greeted by Bethany's scrawling handwriting. It said *Perfect Bucket List*, each letter written with a different crayon. It was so Beth.

Savannah turned the page:

*1. Motorcycle—check*

Bethany had fumbled some sticky tape out of her pocket and glued it onto the back of her Polaroid to stick the picture onto the page.

Savannah looked at her. "I'm not quite sure I understand," she said.

Her reply was a smile and a hand on Savannah's thigh.

"Savy," she said, her thumb stroking Savannah's knee over the fabric of her blue pyjama pants. "This," she pointed at herself in her biker outfit, "is certainly not everything you ever dreamt of. Just because this disease has decided to make you sick doesn't mean we have to let it win, right? It doesn't mean we have to sit here and wait until…you know."

Her gaze fixed on the floor, her mouth apparently not willing to pronounce the words again.

"I love you, Savannah." Bethany looked straight into Savannah's eyes. "I love you, and I want you to live your life to the fullest. I want you to enjoy every second of it."

"And how am I gonna do that?" Savannah whispered, her eyes not once leaving Bethany's crystal-blue gaze.

"By making this list with me. In this book." She smiled. "There are enough pages in it to fill them with the most amazing memories. I want you to write down everything you ever wanted to do in your life. It doesn't matter if it's small or big or silly or adventurous—anything. I promise you we'll do it. I give you my word."

A thick lump formed in her throat at seeing Bethany like this, here in their old living room, on the couch they had picked out together, wearing this crazy but sexy outfit, bringing her all these things, these promises, this book.

And she was looking at her with so much love in her eyes that it made Savannah's heart hurt. She wanted nothing more than to press her lips on Bethany's in that moment, wanted nothing more than to tell her that this would be the first point on her perfect bucket list.

"You want to do that with me?" Bethany asked. Then, in a small, quiet voice, she said, "Or do you think it's stupid?"

"Nothing you ever did for me was stupid, Bethany," Savannah answered and covered Bethany's hand with her own. "But are you sure? This sounds like a lot of work for you to put into this, like it's going to take up a lot of time."

"I'm on a break from work," Bethany explained. "I talked to Patricia today, and I'm not going to go back for now."

Savannah smiled, but the tears in her eyes made her vision blurry. She knew what it meant. Bethany was taking time off work until she'd be gone. She'd take care of her until she was dead, because there wasn't much time left, right? Oh wow. Fuck.

"Savy?" Bethany whispered. Her thumb quickly brushed a tear away from Savannah's eye before it could roll down her cheek. "You okay?"

"Yeah. Yes, I'm okay." Savannah nodded. "Let's do this, then."

"Let's do this!" Bethany repeated and wrapped her arms around Savannah, who was inhaling Bethany's smell. She smelled like hairspray and leather, like the hot biker lady she had always dreamt of when she was younger.

"Thank you," she whispered, and she could feel Bethany smile against the skin of her neck.

Bethany was right. Her life wasn't fucking over. She wasn't going to spend the last few months of her life in front of the TV. Bethany was giving her new hope and new power, and she was going to use it—for both of them.

Savannah Cortez would have a hell of an awesome rest of her life, however long it might be.

# Chapter 8

WATCHING *WILD HOGS* ON THE couch with Bethany was definitely as good as going on a biker tour herself, maybe even better, Savannah decided. And she didn't even like the movie. She hated silly slapstick comedies, especially if they were based on the lives of a bunch of men that were old enough to be her dad. But Bethany was having fun, and she looked stunning. So stunning that Savannah could hardly take her eyes off her.

As much as she had been trying to deny it, the wish to be close to Bethany had become so much stronger in the past few days. It became too hard to ignore it. Impossible.

The thought of Amber and their awkward conversation was still occupying Savannah's thoughts, and she had no idea how to proceed. Should she tell Bethany? Should she warn her? Make a hint? Keep her mouth shut? Tell Bethany to fix things with Amber?

Bethany was stuffing some tortilla chips into her mouth and snorted at one of John Travolta's jokes. *Adorable*. Then Savannah finally cleared her throat. "Beth?"

"Hm?" Bethany answered and held her bowl of chips out to Savannah. "I'm so sorry. I've totally kept them all to myself, so rude."

Savannah smiled. "Thanks, I'm not hungry. I was wondering if you talked to Amber today."

Bethany's hand froze before she could put another one of the salty snacks into her mouth. "No. Why?"

Savannah looked away, absentmindedly ripping the Coke label off the bottle in front of her. "I just wanted to know if you two were okay."

She got a frown in response. "Why wouldn't we be?"

*Because she calls your friends behind your back and acts like a mistrusting bitch.* Savannah bit her lower lip to keep herself from speaking the words out loud. "Because I think..." The Coke label was ripped into a million tiny pieces by now. "I just don't want you to get in trouble for spending so much time with me. I mean, I love it when you're around, but not if it means it'll cause you problems."

The frown on Bethany's forehead only deepened, and she put the bowl on the table to move a little closer to Savannah.

"Savy, why would you think that? She's okay with me being here. She knows we're just friends."

"Oh, does she?" Savannah hissed a little more angrily, her brown eyes getting a bit of their old furious sparkle back. "I wouldn't be too sure." Damn, this wasn't how she had wanted to have this conversation. She didn't want to be the one telling Bethany about the call. She had hoped Amber had been brave enough to do it herself.

"Where is this coming from?" Bethany asked, her voice serious now.

Savannah sighed. "It's not my job to tell you. I didn't want to start this now, I—"

"Did she call you?" Bethany blurted out, her eyelids blinking rapidly.

*Great.* She had told herself *no more lies.* She had to be honest with her. "Yeah. But before you start questioning me, I think you should talk it out with her and not me. All I can say is that she seems pretty insecure and, well, a little jealous."

*Very fucking jealous and completely insecure. But I will spare you the details. You've been through enough.*

Bethany was looking down at her lap, her previous excitement about the movie gone. Savannah wanted to kick herself. "I understand if you want to leave," Savannah started carefully, but Bethany raised her head, a pleading look on her face.

"Honestly, Savy, I don't think I want to handle this tonight. With her, I mean." She sighed. "I'm just so, so sorry that she called you. She shouldn't have done that. None of this is your fault. That's totally inappropriate."

"Beth, it's okay—"

"No, it's not," Bethany interrupted her. "It's not okay that she dragged you into this. And I will handle it, of course. But I've honestly had enough ups and downs today. I kind of just want some quiet."

"Of course."

Bethany looked around the room, then back at Savannah. The light of the television was throwing colourful shadows on their faces, but neither of them was listening to the movie anymore.

"I, um…"

"Mm?"

"Would it be okay if I stayed here tonight?" Bethany asked carefully, and Savannah felt her heart skip a beat. "I mean, not in your bed, of course, but on the couch," Bethany continued. "I don't want to see Amber, but I don't want go home alone either. I can't stand the thought of being alone at the moment."

Savannah nodded, a smile tugging on her lips. "Of course you can stay, Beth—always. And you can have the bed. I can sleep here. I don't mind."

Bethany shook her head vehemently. "No way. I'll take the couch. I like it."

A smile appeared on Savannah's face, but she remained quiet. She knew that Bethany wouldn't accept any other answer right now.

"Let me get you something to sleep in," she said, not able to hide the fact that Bethany spending the night was bringing a happy shade of pink to her cheeks. She knew the circumstances were sad. She knew Bethany was scared of being alone and probably scared of facing her girlfriend, but still, the thought filled Savannah with happy excitement.

Admittedly, she was sort of relieved Bethany had decided to change in the bathroom and not right in front of her. She could have told her that her blue toothbrush was still lying in the drawer under the sink, but it made her feel silly, so she offered her a new one. A yellow one.

While Bethany was getting ready, Savannah prepared the couch and got her biggest pillow out of the bedroom to put on the sofa with a fluffy blanket. She put a bottle of water next to it on the table in case Bethany got thirsty. She closed the curtains so the sunlight wouldn't wake her too early.

Savannah smiled when Bethany returned and took in the sight of her without makeup: her rosy skin, her hair held up in a ponytail, wearing *her* bedclothes. Bethany had worn Savannah's PJs countless times, but it had been so long since she'd last seen her like that.

"Tell me if you need anything, okay?" Savannah told her, about to head to the bedroom.

"Savy?"

"Yes?"

"Would you stay until...until I've fallen asleep?"

Savannah swallowed. "Yes. Of course."

Bethany smiled, tired but thankful. She snuggled up on the couch, dragged the blanket up to her chin and buried her face in the huge pillow.

"Mm," she sighed. "Good night, Savannah."

"Night, Beth-Beth."

It didn't take long for Bethany to fall asleep, which Savannah could tell by the sound of her even breathing, but she didn't want to get up just yet. Bethany looked so peaceful and beautiful.

Savannah's mind travelled back to the events of the day, back to the book, the list. She couldn't imagine a better time to get inspired about what she wanted the rest of her life to look like than now, with Bethany sleeping right next to her.

She sat down in the armchair right by her side, grabbed a piece of paper and a pen, and started thinking.

Bethany woke up to the smell of fresh coffee. She opened her eyes and slowly adjusted to the light in the room. It took her a minute to realize where she was until she finally recognized the unfamiliar, yet so familiar, surroundings.

"Morning," she mumbled and smiled as she spotted Savannah in the kitchen, putting some croissants in the oven.

"Morning, sleepyhead," Savannah laughed and walked over to her. "Did you sleep okay?"

"Yeah. Yeah, I did," Bethany replied honestly. In fact, it was the first morning since she had found out about Savannah's disease that she truly felt rested. "You?"

"Yup. I made a list last night."

Bethany immediately felt wide awake, sat up, and dropped the blanket to the floor.

"Awesome, let me see it!"

"I'll show you over breakfast," Savannah told her and headed back to the kitchen counter to squeeze a few oranges.

It was unusual for Savannah to prepare breakfast. In all those years they had been dating, Savannah had always been the one to sleep late and hide in bed until Bethany would finally wake her up and drag her to the breakfast table. Still, she couldn't deny that she liked waking up to a domesticated Savannah in the kitchen.

Bethany got up and turned on the radio. She liked the song that was playing and couldn't stop herself from dancing into the kitchen—music always had that effect on her.

"So, how long have you been up? You look so fresh and showered and… *awake*." Bethany grinned.

"A little while." Savannah smiled, put the remaining few items on the table, and motioned to Bethany to take a seat.

"Three sugars?"

"Yes, please," Bethany nodded as Savannah poured the coffee into her mug.

Savannah finally sat down across from her and put the steaming croissants on the table. They filled the room with the smell of freshly baked dough. A perfect start to a probably not-so-perfect day. Bethany would worry about that later.

"Here," Savannah said proudly as she shoved a piece of paper over to Bethany.

Bethany took the list, smiling excitedly, to see what her friend had come up with the previous night. She scanned each point on the little paper and couldn't help but frown.

She read it again. And another time. But the disappointment was clearly displaying on her features.

"What?" Savannah raised an eyebrow.

"Nothing. Just—is that really what you want to do? I mean, these are your dreams?"

"What's wrong with them?" Savannah asked, her voice not as happy as before.

"I don't know. I mean, do yoga? Buy a new car?"

"My car is old. I've only ever bought used cars. I want something with all the extras."

Bethany cleared her throat before continuing. "Tidy the spare room and put up new wallpaper. Visit the Iowa Firefighters Memorial Museum.

Eat the veggie lasagne at Toni's Pizza Place," she mumbled, shaking her head with every word that came out of her mouth.

"What?" Savannah shrugged. "I've had a lot of free time on my hands in the past year."

"I don't know, Savy," Bethany started, her voice sad.

"You changed your mind? You don't want to do this anymore?" Savannah crossed her arms in front of her chest.

"Of course I do. I just think it's… I don't know… I thought you had more, well, *exciting* things in mind."

"I think they are exciting, and it's what I want to do."

"Okay," Bethany gave in. "Then we'll do them."

She put the list aside and took her phone out of her pocket to text Amber. Both of them were finishing their breakfast in quiet. "I'm gonna try to meet up with her soon so she and I can talk things out."

"That sounds like a good plan." Savannah got up to clean the breakfast table. "You want to take a shower first?"

"Yeah. Can I borrow a top?" Bethany asked. She didn't want to get back into her biker clothes. Especially not when she was about to meet her girlfriend.

"Sure thing. You know where the closet is. Pick whatever you like."

Bethany nodded and smiled, then headed to the bathroom to get ready. Her head felt empty as she was standing in the shower and letting the hot water rain down on her body. Amber had texted back, had told her to come over to her place whenever she had time. Bethany didn't know what she should expect of the meeting. Should she mention Amber's call right away? She didn't know how much energy she was going to be able to put into this conversation. Her mind was still trying to imagine the next few weeks if all she was going to do with Savannah was learn how to knit or spend money on useless items that she knew Savannah neither really wanted nor needed. These were going to be her last months with her, their last chance to make things as good as possible for her, but it seemed as if Savannah had already given up, as if she saw herself as this sick person who had accepted waiting quietly for her last day.

She turned around so the water was splashing on her face. Her eyes were pressed shut to keep herself from crying. She stood there until her skin turned wrinkly and the feeling in her stomach told her that she wasn't ready to leave and face another disappointing conversation with a woman that meant a lot to her.

When she was finally dressed, Bethany walked back into the living room, where Savannah had started cleaning. She wondered if this was a way for Savannah to distract herself. Savannah, who had always been a very chaotic person, with her clothes thrown all over the furniture and with huge piles of dirty dishes next to the sink, now seemed to be determined to have everything in perfect order. Maybe she needed it, this kind of clarity in her otherwise dark reality.

"Want me to bring that down for you on my way out?" Bethany asked, pointing at the big garbage bag Savannah was tying up.

"That'd be nice, thanks," she replied. She gave her a half smile as she looked at the shirt Bethany was wearing.

"You picked that out for me, remember? It was the day when—"

"When we wanted to visit Joan, and I accidentally spilled my milkshake on your top at McDonald's," Bethany finished for her.

"Yeah."

They smiled at each other before Bethany came a step closer to hug Savannah.

"I'll let you know how it goes," Bethany stated, and Savannah nodded.

"Good luck."

Bethany took the garbage bag and headed out the door before rushing down the steps of the hallway.

Mrs. McPherson was cleaning the stairs with a wet mop. She glared at Bethany as if Bethany's dirty shoes were ruining all of her work. Bethany was about to greet her when she suddenly lost her balance on the slippery floor. She let out a muffled scream as she fell down the last two steps. The garbage bag went flying through the air in slow motion and landed on the floor with a loud thud. The plastic ripped open, and the contents spilled all over the hallway.

"You've got to be kidding me!" Mrs. McPherson yelled angrily, not bothering to ask if Bethany had hurt herself. "You better clean that up!"

Bethany moaned a little as she rubbed her back, which hurt pretty badly from the fall.

"I'm sorry," she mumbled and immediately tried to collect the empty yogurt cups and banana peels that were filling the air with a slightly rotten smell.

"Typical. Always trouble. Always the same," the elderly lady muttered.

Bethany rolled her eyes, not really sure how to get the trash back into the broken bag, let alone carry all of it outside to the garbage bin. Just as she was almost done, something caught her attention. It was a piece of paper with Savannah's handwriting. That alone wouldn't have been too unusual, but she could make out the word "motorcycle" on top, which gave her a vague idea of what she was looking at. She straightened the paper, which was ripped in half, and felt a lump in her throat. The original bucket list.

She didn't have time to read what else was written on the paper as Mrs. McPherson gave her an impatient look and tapped her foot on the floor. There had to be a second half. Where was the second half?

Bethany's heart was beating faster, and she didn't dare look at her ex-neighbor as she spontaneously emptied the whole garbage bag on the floor to dig in it for the second part of the list.

"What on earth do you think you're doing?" the woman shrieked in her red-faced rage.

"Mrs. McPherson, please go back inside and feed your goldfish. I promise you I will clean everything up, and tonight when I'm back, I'm gonna scrub the whole hallway—twice—so clean that you'll be able to eat off of it. Just please leave me alone for a minute."

"Unbelievable. *Un-be-lievable.*"

Bethany let out a relieved sigh when she finally heard the door to her apartment slam shut.

She would smell like trash once she arrived at Amber's place, but she couldn't care less. She kept digging and searching until she found what she was looking for, not able to hold back a loud "thank God!" as she finally held the second piece of paper in her hands.

She held it next to the other one, just to be sure that it was the right one, and quickly stuffed both halves into her jeans pocket. She had no idea why there would be a second list, and she had no idea why Savannah had ripped this one in two and thrown it away, but something told her that it was important.

Maybe something like fate really did exist? Maybe someone up there wanted her to find it?

"New shirt?" The look on Amber's face was cold as she greeted her, and Bethany didn't miss the tone in her question.

Silence.

"It's okay. I know it's hers," Amber told her.

Bethany sighed. "Feels like we haven't talked in a while," she started, not able to hide the insecurity in her voice.

"Well, you were pretty busy," Amber said slowly and sat down at the dining room table.

"You were the one who left early yesterday morning, Ams. It was pretty obvious you didn't want to talk to me."

"It would have made no sense to talk to you about our relationship right before you take Savannah to her doctor's appointment," Amber said. "That's obviously more important."

Bethany nodded. "Yeah it kind of is."

What was Amber implying here? Was that sarcasm in her voice? Bethany couldn't really tell, but it did piss her off. And it pissed her off even more that Amber would call Savannah after such an obviously important and possibly life-altering appointment.

They were staring at each other, and the unusual coldness between them scared Bethany. Amber was such a warm and caring person. What had happened? "I know that you called her, Amber."

Amber let out an ironic laugh. "Of course you do. Of course she would tell you. Why am I not surprised?"

"I sensed it, and I made her tell me. This is not her fault."

"Yeah, I get that you defend her."

"Oh my God," Bethany shook her head. "How can you turn this around now? It was a coward's move to call her. What did you even tell her?"

"I'm sure she already told you all the details, Beth, so don't play stupid."

Bethany's eyes widened at the other woman's words, and she felt herself tear up.

"I'm sorry. I didn't mean it like that," Amber quickly said.

"Okay, then what did you tell her?" Bethany whispered as she pulled at the sleeves of her shirt.

"I asked her if she's still in love with you, Beth."

Bethany felt her heart pound faster in her chest. "And what did she say?" The words had come out faster than intended, more hopeful than intended. She realized how she must have sounded, but it was too late to take it back.

"She hung up. And I don't blame her. It was pretty fucked up to ask her that."

"It was. God, Ams, she had a totally awful morning. The doctors told her again that there was nothing else they could do for her. And you call her and make her feel guilty for something that is absolutely not her fault?"

"I'm sorry, okay? Geez, I'm sorry, but I fucking love you, Bethany. This is messed up. I didn't mean to. You know me. Fuck, you know me, and you know that I don't want to hurt anyone. But losing you? It hurts. It just hurts."

"But you're not losing me. How many times do I have to tell you that?" Bethany blurted out, shocked to see tears in Amber's eyes. She wasn't sure that she had ever seen her cry before.

"I already have."

Bethany gave her a puzzled look when she suddenly spotted the box on the floor behind Amber. She couldn't make out much, just a few shirts she was sure she had seen in her own bathroom a few days before.

"What's this?" she whispered, pointing at it.

"Stuff," Amber breathed out, holding back a sob.

"Are you..." She swallowed. "Are you breaking up with me?"

Amber was looking at her, silent, tears rolling down her cheeks. She reached for her bag to get out her keys, removed one of them from its key ring, and shoved it over the table. The key to Bethany's door.

"Yeah. Yeah, I am." Her voice was shaky but soft. "But I'm only doing what you're too afraid to do."

"But that's not true!" Bethany half yelled, not willing to take the key. "It's not. No!" Her head felt hot. She didn't want to let her do this. How could she do this?

"Beth," Amber started. She tried to smile. "I lost you the moment you saw her again. I know that. And the thing is that this has nothing to do with the fact she's sick. It has nothing to do with the fact that you're scared of losing her and want to spend her last months with her." She reached out to take Bethany's hand, and Bethany grabbed it, not wanting to let go, not wanting to be alone. "It's about the fact that she's your true love. And I come second. I've always come second."

Bethany shook her head. She tried to protest, but no words came out.

"Even before you met her again, she was always going to be the one for you, Beth. I understand that now. And call me selfish, but I want to come first for someone." Amber was smiling sadly and wiped away a tear. "I would love for you to love me the way I love you, but you don't. At least not as strongly. And I'm going to let you go."

The words felt like a knife in Bethany's chest. She quickly pulled her own hand away from Amber's and crossed her arms in front of her chest protectively. Should she fight for her? Would it make sense to fight? Would it be unfair toward Amber to make her change her mind? She didn't know.

"So, are we going to stop talking now? Completely? You'll never call me again?" Bethany asked, desperation in her voice as she tried to hold back a sob.

"I don't know, Beth. I'm sorry. It's just… I don't think I can do this. As much as I want to, and I want to support you as a friend because I know all this is rough for you, but…" It was obvious that words had left her, but it was just as obvious what Amber was trying to say. "I can't do this."

Bethany suddenly knew she was going to be alone. She knew she couldn't hold it against Amber. She couldn't expect her to be more understanding. And fuck, of course she was right. Of course she loved Savannah more than anyone else in this world. And it was probably selfish to expect Amber to accept this and stick around. But she didn't want any of this. She hadn't planned this. She hadn't expected to fall back in love with her ex. She hadn't expected to want a future with the one person it was impossible to have a future with.

Images of the upcoming years were flashing in front of her eyes. Years without Savannah and without Amber. And it scared the shit out of her.

"Okay," Bethany finally whispered. It was all there was left to say. She took the key wordlessly and removed her own key to Amber's apartment from her key ring as she got up from the table.

"Uh, here's a bag for you. With some of your stuff that was still lying around here. If I still find anything else, I will send it to you, of course," Amber said.

Bethany nodded. Tears were blurring her vision.

Amber walked around the table, obviously unsure how to say good-bye. They stood awkwardly in front of each other. Then she took a step forward to wrap her arms around Bethany. Bethany's body stiffened, and she didn't move a muscle while Amber pressed her body close against hers.

"I'm sorry," she whispered into the fabric of Bethany's shirt, and Bethany closed her eyes, feeling entirely lost.

She turned around on her heel, as she was not willing to look into Amber's eyes again before she walked out the door. The weight of the bag felt so heavy in her hands, as if it were about to slip out of her fingers. It seemed to have become a theme. Everything was about to slip out of her hands. And there wasn't much she could do about it.

Her apartment felt empty when she stepped inside. Bethany had no idea what to do with herself and suppressed her tears with everything she had. She had cried too much in these past weeks.

Amber had been the one to make her smile again after her breakup with Savannah. She had been the first person to make her feel loved again, to make her feel safe when she had been so lost. And now here she was, having lost another person that had meant so much to her.

Her head was throbbing, and she popped in two painkillers, which she downed with a glass of water.

What was she supposed to do? She couldn't go to work to distract herself since she had quit in order to take care of Savy. To do a bunch of things on a list that she knew meant nothing to Savannah.

The list!

Her heart started beating faster when she remembered what was still waiting in her jeans pocket. She had completely forgotten about it over all this emotional turmoil with Amber.

Bethany carefully pulled the two pieces of paper out of her pocket and searched with nervous impatience for some tape to glue the list together.

It still smelled of garbage. Though the paper was dirty, the words were still readable.

1. Motorcycle—check

Underneath were several more points, and Bethany slowly started reading and imagining Savannah's face as she wrote down all of her ideas the previous night.

2. Design my own tattoo.

3. Feed a koala.

4. Learn to tie a knot in a cherry stem using only my tongue.

(Bethany had to laugh.)

5. Paint my front door red.

6. Be in two places at once.

7. Spend the night at an aquarium.

8. Get a pink Christmas tree.

She felt her heart grow a little warmer. Those things were cute. Somehow, it was so unlike Savannah to have such adorable wishes, but somehow, it fitted her perfectly. Somehow, they sounded like things she herself would put on her bucket list.

9. Steal a school bus.

10. Have sex in a hammock between palm trees.

"Oh dear, Savy." Bethany laughed and shook her head.

11. Own a tiger.

12. See the New York Jets win the Super Bowl.

13. Ride in a stretch limo and drink fancy champagne.

14. Let go of a floating lantern and make a wish.

Bethany was still smiling, though she didn't quite understand why Savannah would possibly rip this list in two and replace it with the most boring bucket list imaginable. Sure, a few wishes would be harder to realize than others, but they would try. Why not accept a little challenge?

She kept reading, when suddenly she felt a knot in her chest.

15. Swim with a dolphin.

16. Kiss underneath a rainbow.

17. Kiss in front of the Eiffel Tower.

(Those were dreams they used to have together, weren't they?)

18. See the July 4th fireworks on a helicopter with the woman I love.

Bethany swallowed.

19. Go to Machu Picchu.

20. Have a girls' night out with the Trashy Triplets.

She felt herself tear up. To anyone else, this list would probably seem insignificant, but Bethany knew what it meant. She knew what every single word meant. And she knew how alone Savannah must have been feeling.

She wanted to see their friend Joan again before she died. The three of them used to call themselves the *Trashy Triplets* back in high school because they were inseparable.

She knew Savannah wanted to do all these romantic things and probably felt silly asking for them. Bethany wished she could hug her right this second.

21. Apologize to my parents.

22. Talk to my grandmother one more time.

Bethany's thumb was running along the paper, and she could see it was wavy at some spots where it had gotten wet and where the ink was slightly smeared. She knew tears must have fallen on it and she was doing her best not to add any of her own.

She could see there was supposed to be one more point. It started with a *B*, but then Savannah must have stopped writing.

*B*? What did she want to say?

Whatever it was, it was probably what had made her rip up the list in the end. It was probably the final wish that Savannah knew she didn't want to ask for.

Part of her felt mad. Well, maybe not mad. Sad. Sad that Savannah would have kept this from her. That she would have decided to go through with those entirely unimportant wishes just because she was too proud or too embarrassed to admit what she really wanted.

Bethany shook her head, not letting go of the piece of paper in her hands that suddenly meant the world to her.

"No," she mumbled. "No, Savannah Cortez. I won't let you get away that easily."

And with that, she was out of the apartment.

Savannah's eyes widened at the sound of someone hammering against her door.

"Open!" She heard a familiar voice yell from outside. She frowned.

"Beth?" she asked, confused. Savannah opened the door to let her friend storm inside. "What's wrong?" Savannah asked. "Did something happen?"

"Yes. Yes, something happened," Bethany told her, out of breath.

Savannah had to grin at the sight of Bethany's dirty clothes.

"Somehow you always manage to ruin my shirts, don't you?" she said. "What did you fall into?"

"I fell into your garbage, Savannah."

"Um, okay?" What was this all about? "And what did Amber say?"

"We'll talk about that later."

"All right. What else do you want to talk about?"

Savannah couldn't help but feel a little worried. She wasn't able to analyze the expression on Bethany's face. She looked a little stressed out and also a little angry? Did Amber say anything to her? Had she done something wrong? She couldn't think of anything.

"I want to talk about why you're acting so stupid, Savannah."

"Excuse me?" Savannah blurted out, not understanding the world anymore. "What on earth did I do?"

Bethany didn't say anything, just put the list on the table forcefully.

"Oh my God. How did you…" Savannah shook her head. She felt the heat rise in her body, felt her cheeks turn red. This couldn't be true. This was scary. How high were the chances of Bethany finding it? Next to nothing!

"It doesn't really matter how. What matters is that you would rather visit a firefighter memorial museum with me than do the things that are really important to you. What the hell were you thinking?"

"I don't know, what was I thinking?" Savannah looked away. "This was just a silly first draft, Beth. Silly things that can't come true anyways. I wasn't thinking straight."

"You obviously weren't when you decided to rip up this thing and throw it away," Bethany concluded, her voice still upset.

"You weren't supposed to see this," Savannah murmured.

Bethany put her hand on her hip, a challenging look on her face. "I wasn't supposed to see what you really want your life to look like? I wasn't supposed to see what you feel? I wasn't supposed to see what would make you happy? Explain that logic to me, please—but oh wait, don't! Because it's the same logic you used when you decided to break up with me and not tell me that you're sick. It's the same damn logic—and here I was, thinking we were past this!"

Savannah felt guilty, but what was she supposed to tell her? Was she supposed to tell her that basically every point on that list was missing a *with you* at the end? Let go of a floating lantern and make a wish with you? Wish that we'll be together forever? Paint my front door red because it's what your favourite couple on *One Tree Hill* did—and I thought I'd do the same for you? Kiss you in front of the Eiffel Tower? Spend the night at an aquarium with you? Get a pink Christmas tree because you always wanted one and I never allowed it? The list basically screamed "be with me!"

Oh screw this, she didn't want to cry again. "I'm sorry," she said instead.

Bethany took a step closer. "Savannah," she whispered and took her hand. "Don't think I don't understand what it means. Because I do. And I want all of this. I want to do all of this with you." She smiled. "Even if some of those things are illegal, I think?"

A smile tugged at Savannah's lips. "A few of those points are impossible, though."

"Nothing is impossible," Bethany corrected her and shook her head. "We'll make it possible." With that, she let a bag drop on the table.

"What's this?" Savannah asked carefully before peeking inside. What she saw made her laugh.

Cherries.

"Oh dear," Savannah mumbled and put the little red fruit on a plate.

"It was the only thing I could still make possible tonight," Bethany explained. "It can't be that hard, can it?" she grinned.

Savannah shook her head. "We better start trying."

Three hours later, both of them were sitting on the floor, surrounded by cherry pits, their bellies hurting from all the laughter and all the fruit.

"Look! It totally counts!" Savannah insisted as she held up a rather pathetic looking "knot" in the stem.

"Yeah, I think that's okay." Bethany chuckled.

"Oh screw this, I'm sure my tongue's gonna hurt in the morning. It's not used to that much action anymore," Savannah added with a wink.

Bethany was looking at her, and Savannah thought she could see her blush. She looked adorable. Somehow her legs had ended up on Bethany's lap during the whole cherry debacle, and she felt a sudden wave of heat rush through her body. Bethany made her so happy. And she still didn't know what had gone down with Amber today.

"So, are you gonna tell me what happened today?" Savannah asked carefully.

Instantly, Bethany looked down at her lap. Her hands were resting on Savannah's jeans. "It's over," she said slowly, and Savannah was glad she was done eating cherries, or she probably would have choked on one of the pits.

"Over? Oh my God. Beth, I am so sorry. I don't know what to say. Are you okay?" She wasn't sorry that Amber was gone. She wasn't sorry that Bethany wasn't going to sleep with another woman every night anymore. But she was sorry for her. She didn't want her to hurt. It was the last thing she wanted.

Bethany looked at her, and she could see the sadness in her eyes. "I'm okay as long as I'm with you," Bethany admitted, and Savannah closed her eyes at those words.

"I'll be okay as long as I have you. But I don't know what will happen after that."

Savannah swallowed. It would always be like this, wouldn't it? These extreme mood swings. From lying on the floor, laughing, to lying on the floor, crying. She could feel Bethany's hand lying heavily on her leg. She could feel her eyes drilling into her. She didn't know what to do. She knew what she wanted to do, but it wasn't right to do it, was it? Not right after their breakup.

They were staring at each other, and Savannah felt the tension in every fiber of her body. All she needed to do was lean over. They were already so close. All it would take was a few inches, and she would feel her. Her gaze lingered on Bethany, on her lips, then up to those clear blue eyes. It made Savannah shiver.

"I'm always here for you. You know that, right? As long as I can be," she whispered.

"Yes, I know. It's one of the few things I know for sure." Bethany was squeezing Savannah's leg and smiled at her when suddenly someone started knocking at the door.

"What the fuck?" Savannah looked at Bethany questioningly. "That's not Amber, is it?"

"God no, I doubt it," Bethany replied. They both scrambled to their feet. Savannah moved over to the door and opened it to see who the annoying intruder was.

"Mrs. McPherson," she said, confused. "What are you doing here?"

"Where is your girlfriend?" the elderly woman asked angrily.

"I don't have a g—"

"I'm here," Bethany interrupted her and softly pushed Savannah aside.

"You said you would scrub the hallway. You promised me. And look at it—it's still a complete mess. I am *not* going to clean up those disgusting pudding stains and whatever else you left there, Bethany. I am *not* your cleaning lady!"

Bethany sighed and gave Savannah an apologetic look. "I'll be right back, okay?"

Savannah nodded. She smiled sympathetically as she was stroking Bethany's arm. "Okay. Do you need help?"

"No, I've got it. But I expect to find a perfect knot when I come back," she told her with a wink.

Savannah laughed. She closed the door behind Bethany and examined the mess on the living room floor. This was why she loved her. She missed it. The chaos.

She walked over to the table and looked at the battered list before taking a pen and the Polaroid camera. She smiled as she took a picture of the little knot and shook it until the image showed up. She glued it into her book carefully before writing another number next to it.

2. Learn to tie a knot in a cherry stem, using only my tongue—check.

# Chapter 9

She first looked at herself in the mirror, then at her watch, then back at her reflection.

"Do we really need the leather gloves, Beth?" Savannah asked. Bethany was throwing a bunch of things into her black backpack.

"Do you want to leave fingerprints?" Bethany asked without waiting for an answer. "Of course we need them!"

Savannah frowned and straightened her tight black sweatshirt over her equally tight black leggings. Her makeup was dark for dramatic flair. Bethany had suggested wearing Catwoman masks, but Savannah had told her this might be going a step too far.

It was 2:00 a.m., and the streets were empty when they stepped out of the house, careful not to make any noise in the hallway. Bethany was about to walk straight to her car when Savannah grabbed her arm.

"You insist on wearing leather gloves, but then you want to take the car? Where do you want to park it without being noticed? In the garage? Or do you plan to switch it for the bus and leave it there until we come back?"

Bethany's eyes widened as she took in Savannah's words, and Savannah had to chuckle.

"You're cute."

Their destination wasn't too far away, so Bethany and Savannah walked in the cool November air. Even though they had spent every day together in the past two weeks, planning to steal the school bus tonight had been rather spontaneous. Bethany had insisted that they do it tonight, even though Savannah was still trying to convince her friend that she shouldn't commit any crimes and possibly get in trouble for her stupid bucket list.

Savannah had suggested they wait until the very end with this particular wish, because it would be hard to finish the bucket list in jail—but once again Bethany's answer was, "Trust me."

And Savannah did trust her. She always had. They finally arrived at the huge garage where the school buses were kept, and Savannah swallowed. This was a bad idea, wasn't it?

"How are we going to get in, Beth? Do you have anything in your bag to crack open locks? Should we break a window? Wait in the bushes until someone magically shows up and unlocks the gate?"

"Um..." Bethany mumbled, chewing on her bottom lip. "Wait here and let me handle that." Then she ran to the other side of the garage.

"Hey!" Savannah hissed. "You can't leave me here!"

She tried to keep up, but Bethany was much faster than her, and Savannah quickly felt out of breath. When she finally arrived at the rear of the garage, Bethany was holding a window open with a triumphant smile.

"How on earth did you do that?" Savannah gave Bethany a dubious glare.

Bethany winked and climbed through the small window into the garage. She landed safely on her feet and turned around, grinning.

She held her arms open. "Jump! I'll catch you," she whispered.

Savannah still felt dubious but finally let out a sigh as she let her body slide off the edge of the window and landed in Bethany's arms.

They stumbled backward a little as Savannah's feet hit the ground, but Bethany had her arms wrapped securely around her. They stood like that for a moment, smiling shyly, and then Bethany finally let Savannah out of her embrace.

"That wasn't so hard, was it?" she said.

"I can't believe we're doing this," Savannah mumbled, though she had to admit the whole experience was thrilling. Pretty much exactly how she had always pictured it.

Savannah had always imagined herself to be the one plotting this adventure, but as it turned out, Bethany was—once again—full of surprises.

She looked around the hall to examine the five big yellow buses with a smirk.

"So, which one is it gonna be?" she asked while slowly taking a step closer to one of the vehicles.

"I think this one looks—"

"That one!" Bethany interrupted her and headed straight to the bus standing at the far end of the hall.

"Uh, okay." Savannah followed her. Bethany had already opened the passenger side door to hop inside. She held out her hand to help Savannah climb into the bus next to her, and they both stared at the steering wheel a little helplessly.

"I think it's time to start the engine, Savy. Think our YouTube crash course on how to start a car without keys was actually helpful?"

Savannah nodded. "Two of my cousins are in jail for stealing cars. I guess it can't be that hard." She looked underneath the steering wheel. Then she tried to remove the plastic shield that was protecting the electronics. "So let's play a bit with these wires to cause a short circuit, and this baby will be ours in no time!"

Bethany stared at Savannah and started chewing on her lower lip.

"Savy?"

"Hm?"

"Isn't this, like…dangerous? What if you get electrocuted?"

"Nah," Savannah waved her off before kneeling on the bus's floor to grab the wires. She was just about to put the two ends together when Bethany grabbed her shoulder.

"Stop!" she yelled, her face pale.

"What?" Savannah asked. "We have to. How else do you want to get this thing out of here? Push it? Steal a few horses and turn this into a big yellow carriage?" She loved Bethany, but they could forget the whole thing if they didn't get this engine running very soon.

"That'd be really cute," Bethany smiled. "But no, we could just…" She cleared her throat before putting her hand into the pocket of her jacket. "We could just take the key?" She pulled out a set of car keys.

Savannah stared at her like a deer in headlights. "What's that? Where did you get those?"

"I, um, well, found them? I guess?"

Savannah shook her head. "You're the worst liar ever, Beth. Seriously. Where did you get them?"

"I talked one of the drivers into lending me one for today. That's why it couldn't be any other day, because the school is on holiday." Bethany looked guilty. "Are you mad?"

Savannah sighed. "You could have told me. Did he also leave the garage window open for you?"

Bethany nodded and shifted awkwardly. "I wanted it to look like we really stole it." She pouted. "But I also didn't want you to get arrested. Or fried." She pointed at the wires.

"I can't believe they actually let you borrow a bus, though," Savannah said. "That's crazy. What did you pay them?"

"Nothing," Bethany replied casually. "I can be very persuasive." She shrugged.

For a moment, Savannah was worried Bethany might have, well, *impressed* the guy with her female charms, and she cringed uncomfortably at the image. Then another thought hit her.

She had been honest, hadn't she? Bethany hated lying. She had probably told those people that it was the last wish of her dying friend, and they had pitied her, right? This was no bus-stealing adventure. This was a goddamn pity party. A charity event. Savannah felt a lump in her throat.

"You really are mad," Bethany said softly, and Savannah felt her insides turn mushy at the sound of her sad voice.

Oh God, how could she even consider complaining about this? How could she? Bethany had arranged a goddamned school bus for her, and they were about to go on a freaking road trip! And Savannah didn't even know for sure *how* Bethany had gotten the keys. She didn't want to know because it didn't matter. What mattered was that the woman she loved was about to drive into the sunrise with her in a giant yellow bus and that they would spend the whole day together.

Savannah shook her head as the smile returned to her lips.

"No, Beth. I'm not mad. I think you're amazing. And we're still pretty badass for doing this. I've never driven a bus, and I'm not sure I can do it."

"I can do it," Bethany offered happily. "And you take the map and give me directions. You know I find maps confusing. We'd probably never get there if the roles were reversed."

"Sounds good," Savannah grinned. "I'll open the gate. Get that thing started."

Bethany smiled and tried to push the key into the ignition lock. She pushed again and again—but nothing happened.

"It doesn't fit!" Bethany whined.

Savannah tried it herself and quickly realized that this was indeed not the right key.

"Bummer," Savannah mumbled. "Are you sure we're in the right bus?"

"He said to take the one on the very left." Bethany pouted, and Savannah chuckled.

"Come on," she said as she took Bethany's hand in hers. "Let's try the bus on the other left."

They had a long trip ahead of them. Savannah figured there was at least eight hours of driving left.

The sun was already visible on the horizon and Bethany had been driving for three hours straight now. At first it had been a little bumpy, but Bethany soon got used to the big vehicle. She looked rather tiny behind the huge steering wheel, and Savannah kept smiling at the image she presented next to her.

Bethany had removed her ponytail so her blonde hair was waving lightly in the cool breeze that came in through the opened windows. The radio signal was bad, so they were listening to one of the old mix tapes they had found in a small box under the seat.

Sheryl Crow's "If It Makes You Happy" was playing, and Savannah closed her eyes for a moment. She sat back comfortably in the passenger seat, breathing in the fresh air, and casually put up her feet on the dashboard in front of her. If spending time with Bethany on the road in a more or less stolen bus in the early morning hours was making her happy, then nothing could be that bad, right? Because it didn't matter how much time they would have left as long as she felt as carefree as she was feeling right in this moment.

"Savy, I think we're running out of gas," Bethany said after a while.

"Then you better find a gas station while I get out of this smooth criminal outfit." Savannah smiled. She had decided to change into some other shirt she had brought with her because two girls in a big bus, dressed entirely in black, might make a few people suspicious.

She stood to go change a little further in the back.

She removed the black top and was standing in her bra when she thought she could feel Bethany's gaze on her. She risked a short glance over her shoulder and met Bethany's eyes in the rearview mirror.

"Focus on the road, please," Savannah smirked, causing a rosy blush to creep on Bethany's cheeks.

Savannah tried to play it down, to be flirty, but she had to admit that Bethany watching her change made her feel slightly uncomfortable. Not because she didn't trust her or didn't love her, but simply because her body didn't make her feel confident about herself anymore.

No one had touched her since their breakup. No one had looked at her except for her doctors. No one else had laid eyes on what Savannah had to see every morning in the mirror: a thin, sick, and unattractive woman.

The thought of Bethany possibly finding her undesirable made her want to disappear.

Hell, even Savannah herself wouldn't desire this new version of her. She knew exactly how pretty and attractive she used to be, and had always known how to be flirty and confident, but none of that attitude was left. She hadn't even touched herself in months, often too disgusted by her own condition or too numb from her medication.

Savannah felt relieved when Bethany finally spotted a small gas station at the side of the road.

Bethany quickly changed into a normal outfit as well while Savannah tried to figure out where the gas cap was located.

"Well, well, well." An elderly man with a gray mustache popped up right behind her.

"What are you young ladies doing here in the early morning hours, all alone in an ol' school bus?" he asked Savannah with a strong southern accent.

Bethany peeked out. "We stole it," she whispered proudly, causing the man to frown and twirl the stray hairs of his mustache with his fingers.

Savannah's eyes widened. "We didn't, actually, so no need to call the cops."

"Uh-huh," the man muttered as he walked back to the small shop where he sold drinks and snacks.

She tried to focus on filling the tank with gas, but she felt dizzy. This often happened when she hadn't lain down for a while or when she had to handle stressful situations. She kept her eyes on the gas pump, but her vision was blurry. The pain in her upper stomach was becoming almost unbearable. Wave after wave of nausea kept shaking through her body.

"Are you okay? Savy?" She heard Bethany's voice as if it were coming from miles away. "Savannah?"

"Yeah. I'm… I think I need to use the bathroom," she said, before throwing up right next to the bus.

Savannah lay with her head on Bethany's lap on a couch in the back of the gas station. Bethany was stroking her hair and felt terribly scared and guilty. It was too much for Savannah, wasn't it? She had underestimated her disease, and it made her feel awful to see her like that. *I shouldn't have pushed her to do this.*

"Want some more water?" the elderly man asked Savannah as he sat down on a chair beside them. His name was Joe.

"Thank you," Bethany replied as she took the bottle from him and helped Savannah take a sip.

"It'll be okay. I'm fine. I just feel a little nauseous sometimes," Savannah assured them. "Will you get me my meds?"

Bethany nodded. She knew she didn't need to tell Savannah how she really felt. How much it terrified her. Everything.

She watched Savannah swallow each pill and studied her face to make out if she was in pain. Savannah's features were tense, but she brought out a smile—always the tough one.

"We can go back," she said. "We can call a doctor. I don't know, I'm sure there are doctors around here. We—"

"No," Savannah interrupted her. "I'm good, Beth. I'm good. We won't go home."

"Okay," Bethany whispered, and Savannah got up from her lap.

"I'd like to use the restroom. I need to clean up a little," Savannah mumbled. "Then we can go on."

"It's right outside. The little blue cabin," Joe told her. "Want me to show it to ya?"

"I got it."

Joe cleared his throat. "So, what is this road trip all about, if you don't mind me asking?" he asked when Savannah was out of the room. "I've worked at this godforsaken gas station for over thirty-five years, but never have I met two pretty young ladies alone in a school bus." He cracked open a beer. What time was it? Eight in the morning?

"We're on our way to Copperhill, Tennessee. It was her birthday wish," Bethany lied, trying to avoid Joe's gaze.

Joe nodded slowly and scratched the stubble on his chin.

"Cancer is a bitch," he finally said, and Bethany started choking on her water.

"What do you mean?" *He must be psychic or a wizard.*

"Sweetheart, it's not hard to see that your friend is sick. I lost my dear Carol to that son-of-a-bitch of a disease, and let me tell ya, if God really exists, he and I are gonna have a serious talk if I ever get to meet him."

Bethany swallowed. She hoped Savannah was going to stay in the bathroom for a little while longer. Bethany was sure she wouldn't approve of this kind of conversation.

"I'm sorry about your wife," she whispered.

"Thanks. You know, life isn't fair. But we have to make the best of it. I know she's in a better place now."

He took another sip of his beer and stretched his legs.

"I think it's great that you two are doing what you feel like doing, ya know? What's the point in sitting at home and feeling sorry for yourself when you can go out and enjoy the day? Yeah, the world can be an ugly place, but there's a lot more than that. If I could turn back time, I'd do all kinds of crazy things with Carol. Go camping in the wilderness, make love to her under the stars, ya know?"

Bethany nodded and, despite everything, felt a smile blooming on her lips.

"And you, kiddo," he said, his voice more serious. "You're gonna be all right. You're young."

Bethany gave him a dubious look.

"Look at me. I'm an old fart, but I'm not sad or feeling sorry for myself. I got to spend so many years of my life married to the woman I love, and I know she's not really gone. It doesn't feel like she's gone. I still talk to her, and it still feels like she's listening. And I'm pretty damn sure I'll see her again sooner or later."

"But she's too young to...to..."

"I know," Joe told Bethany, not waiting for her to say the word. "I know, kiddo. And I'm sorry. But you two are gonna make the best of it. She seems like a tough young woman to me. She's not gonna leave you without fighting. She's gonna stay with you for as long as she can, and you're gonna have a hell of a good time. A time you'll always remember. That's something that no one can ever take away from you."

Bethany nodded again and quickly brushed away the tears from her cheeks as she heard Savannah's footsteps in the hallway.

Then the door swung open.

"I'm ready if you are," Savannah said as she came back inside and Bethany quickly got up.

Joe walked with them to their bus and handed them two cans of beer.

"On the house," he told them with a grin. "Have a good trip. Oh, and just follow the road signs to Chattanooga, that's the quickest way."

Savannah nodded as she took the beer, thanking him for his help.

Before Bethany climbed back into the vehicle, she placed a quick kiss on Joe's cheek.

"Thank you," she whispered and gave him a heartfelt smile.

Bethany could still see Joe in the rearview mirror, watching them with a smile on his lips.

Bethany told Savannah she should sleep for a while to regain some energy. Savannah tried to argue at first.

"No. You need to rest. I can follow the road signs for Chattanooga easily enough."

That was almost six hours ago, and Bethany was proud of herself. It wouldn't take much longer to finally get to Copperhill.

Savannah looked peaceful as she slept, and Bethany was glad that the color had returned to her cheeks.

The mix tape was playing some old Patsy Cline song, and the country music fitted the landscape around them perfectly. Bright rays of sunlight were warming her face, yet Bethany thought she could hear the rumble of thunder a few miles away. She took a look over her shoulder and realized there were thick, black clouds in the sky behind them. For a minute, she felt thankful that they were driving a bus and not riding a motorcycle.

Bethany's mind went back to the list and all the things they were still about to do. She was smiling at the thought of making a few of the more difficult wishes come true. It was a little like playing fairy godmother.

The thunder seemed to be getting closer, and Bethany looked at Savannah again, hoping that it wouldn't wake her up. She needed the rest. Maybe she could manage the whole way by herself. Savannah would be happy if they had arrived at their destination when she woke up.

A wave of panic hit Bethany when raindrops started landing on her windshield. She had no clue how to turn on the wipers. She pressed a few buttons, shifted a few levers, but she only managed to turn on the heater and the high beams.

She let out a frustrated groan and decided it was safer to stop at the side of the road until the rain shower had passed.

Savannah still hadn't woken up. Bethany parked the bus and let her head rest on the window next to her to watch the raindrops smash against the glass. First she was lost in thought, but then something caught her attention.

"Savy?" she yelled while poking her friend. "Savy, wake up!"

Savannah moaned a little, then slowly opened her eyes. "What happened?" she asked. "Are we there yet?"

"Not quite yet."

"Did we get lost?"

"No, Savy. Get up."

Savannah wiped the sleep out of her eyes and stared at Bethany, who had pushed the door open and hopped right into the rain.

"Are you insane? You're gonna get a cold," Savannah told her. "Come back inside."

"No, Savannah. Come outside! Just do it!"

Savannah sighed and shook her head as she opened the passenger door and stepped out in the cool November rain.

"And now?" she asked Bethany a little impatiently. "It's raining. Great."

"Turn around!" Savannah did just that. Then she spotted it. The huge rainbow. Double rainbow, even. Bethany thought she could see Savannah blush.

They were in the middle of nowhere, surrounded by corn fields. On their left, the sun was shining brightly. On the right, the sky was painted in a dark gray, almost black. In front of the dark clouds, the giant rainbow was shining in all its beautiful colours. It looked amazing.

Their clothes were already soaked now, but Bethany didn't notice it anymore. She looked at Savannah, who kept staring at the rainbow, then turned around to meet her eyes.

"It's, um, it's a rainbow."

"Yeah," Savannah cleared her throat. "Yeah, I can see that."

Bethany was kicking some small stones away with her foot and stared at the grass underneath her feet. She shrugged.

"Well, I mean, you said you wanted to...you said you wanted a kiss."

Savannah bit her lower lip and nodded slowly. "I guess that's what I said."

"I'm sorry," Bethany stuttered.

"Sorry about what?"

"That I'm the only one around right now. You can, of course, wait for another rainbow. With somebody else, I mean. I don't expect you to... I don't know if you want to, like, maybe some other day."

Savannah closed her eyes and shook her head as she smiled.

"Shut up," she told her, her eyes teary as she opened them again. "Shut up, Beth."

Bethany felt the heart pump faster in her chest as she saw Savannah walk over to her. Her hair was wet, just like her own, and thick raindrops were running down her skin. Her brown eyes looked a little darker than usual.

Then their faces were only inches apart.

For a second, Bethany thought she could see Savannah hesitate, could sense how nervous she was, but a moment later, it was all forgotten. A moment later, everything felt right.

Savannah's lips were on her own, softly at first, brushing lightly against hers. Bethany pulled away a little to search Savannah's eyes for confirmation. She saw the smile on her lips. Saw the relief. The happiness.

Then their lips touched again, and it felt as if nothing had changed. As if they had never broken up. As if they had only been apart for a long vacation and one of them had finally returned home.

All the waiting. All those months. All those nights.

Bethany parted her lips instinctively and caught her breath as she felt the tip of Savannah's tongue against her own. She had missed this taste so much. This feeling. Everything about her.

She could feel Savannah's hand in her hair, could feel her stroke some wet strands out of her face. It was a small gesture that made her heart beat even faster.

This was it. She knew it. This was the moment that changed everything. After this kiss, she wouldn't be able to go back. Savannah would be hers again, because she knew Savannah felt it too. She had to.

Savannah's hand was on her neck now. She pulled her closer, and they deepened the kiss while their bodies and their soaked clothes pressed impossibly close together.

Bethany's eyes were pressed shut, and she felt like never opening them again. It was one of those rare moments in life that you didn't want to end. One of those moments that felt as if someone had lifted a terribly heavy weight off your shoulders that you had forgotten you were carrying all these months.

She never wanted to get used to it again. She never wanted to be without those kisses again.

"I missed you," she gasped as they interrupted the kiss for a second. "I missed you so much. I can't tell you how much."

Savannah nodded, smiling. "Me too," she whispered. "Me too."

Bethany took off her jacket and wrapped it around Savannah as she kissed her once more, smiling against her mouth as she pressed her lips on hers. She lifted her off the ground and twirled her around a little, not once breaking the kiss.

Savannah was so light. Bethany thought she could probably carry her all the way to Copperhill.

She had no idea how long they had been kissing with the jacket held over their heads like a tent. They only stopped when Savannah shivered in her embrace.

"We should get back inside and warm up. I found the button for the heater," Bethany said, smiling while her forehead rested against Savannah's.

"Beth?"

"Hm?" Bethany sighed happily.

"Beth, we forgot to take a picture. For the book."

Bethany pulled away a little and grinned playfully.

"Such a shame. What are we gonna do about that?"

Savannah smiled, laughed even, and her eyes were glowing.

"I'd say you better get that camera out here so that we can, you know, repeat the whole thing. Just for the picture, of course."

Bethany smiled brightly.

"Whatever the lady commands."

The rest of the journey, they couldn't stop smiling.

They didn't talk much, because there wasn't much to say. But it was amazing to enjoy each other's presence like this, with the taste of the other still lingering on their lips.

When they finally saw the Copperhill road sign, Bethany let out an excited squeak.

"We made it, Savy! We actually made it. We're so good!" she chanted and squeezed Savannah's hand a little harder.

"*You* are good, Beth. I slept for a few hours, and you made it all on your own." Savannah smiled.

Bethany blushed. Savannah made her feel so good about herself. She was one of the few people in her life who had always believed in her.

It was almost eleven o'clock, definitely time for a late breakfast or brunch. Since it was a regular work day, the small town didn't seem too crowded. They found a parking lot that was big enough to park the bus and started looking for a nice little diner.

They walked along the streets hand in hand, and Bethany eagerly took in her surroundings. It was a beautiful day, with no more signs of rain, and Savannah Cortez was beside her, their fingers entangled.

It didn't take long for them to find a café where they enjoyed some toast and eggs with a warm cup of coffee, and Bethany knew that this was what she wanted. This. For the rest of her life. Go out for breakfast with this gorgeous woman in front of her.

The cancer felt unreal. Like a bad memory of a stupid nightmare.

Right now, it didn't feel as if anything were about to change. It felt like the start of something great, not like the beginning of the end. As if they had all the time in the world.

After they finished their brunch, they continued their little walk, full and satisfied, until they finally spotted what they had been looking for, the reason for this whole trip.

"There it is!" Savannah told Bethany. "Exciting!" she added with a wink.

On the street in front of them was a long blue line painted on the asphalt. The official border between Georgia and Tennessee.

With a big smile, they reached the line, then followed it all the way until they reached a long bridge with a big, old green sign in front of it:

*Ga. / Tenn. State Line—At this steel bridge, the*
*Toccoa River becomes the Ocoee River.*

Bethany looked at Savannah and grinned.

"We're gonna be in two places at once and above two different rivers at the same time, Savy. How awesome is that, hm?"

"Very awesome," Savannah agreed. "Come on!"

Savannah dragged Bethany with her by the arm as she started running toward the bridge.

Bethany giggled and followed her with fast steps until they were standing on the middle of the bridge.

"Got the cam?" Bethany asked, and Savannah quickly got out the Polaroid.

"Know what I think?" she added.

"What do you think?"

"It'd be even better if we kissed in two places at once," Bethany told her before biting her lower lip.

Savannah laughed.

"Oh, I like the sound of that!" She held up the camera in front of them.

Bethany closed her eyes and sighed contently as Savannah's lips found hers. *Click.*

She made a mental note in her head to scratch out the points on the list as soon they got back to the car.

3. Steal a school bus—check.

4. Kiss underneath a rainbow—check.

5. Kiss in two places at once—check.

# Chapter 10

IT WAS STILL DARK OUTSIDE. December had come, and it was getting colder every day. Savannah heard the wind rattling against her bedroom window and moved a little closer to Bethany, who was sleeping next to her in bed.

The red lights of her radio alarm clock illuminated the room just enough to make out the silhouette of her sleeping girlfriend.

Yeah. Girlfriend. Savannah figured she could call her that again.

Bethany was shifting a little on the mattress, and sometimes Savannah wondered if Bethany could feel her eyes on her. It was as if she were unconsciously trying to wake up whenever Savannah looked at her for a little longer, as if her senses were on full alert and her body was trying to wake up to be there for her.

When Bethany's eyes fluttered open, Savannah kissed her forehead.

"Sleep some more. It's early."

Bethany came closer and nuzzled her head against Savannah's chest. Then she wrapped an arm around her thin body.

"But you're awake too," she whispered as her fingertips were slowly stroking up and down Savannah's bare arm.

Savannah sighed. Her chin was resting on Bethany's head, and blonde hair was tickling her lips. She enjoyed being close to her. She enjoyed it so much because it felt so right to lie next to her; but something inside her kept holding her back.

Their trip in the not-so-stolen bus had been wonderful, and kissing Bethany had made Savannah happier than she had been in a very long time. But Savannah had been scared to take their relationship any further, and she couldn't even explain why. It wasn't that Bethany had tried to push anything. They had cuddled and had kissed every day, had stroked each other softly before falling asleep together, but Savannah had made sure to keep her clothes on.

She did want Bethany. She did want to feel her. But she wanted things to be as they used to be. She wanted to be the person she once was, not the woman she was now.

"I like the sound of the wind," Bethany told her as she began kissing her fingertips. "It makes me want to stay cuddled up in bed with you all day."

"Mm," Savannah mumbled, and her heart beat faster.

What would it mean to sleep with her again? It would bring them so much closer. It would make things so much harder. Make it so much harder to let go.

Savannah could feel Bethany breathe against her neck, could feel her press herself even closer against her body.

The sound of the wind became louder, just like the sound of her own heartbeat in her ears. It felt as if Bethany were surrounding her completely. Her hands were slowly wandering up Savannah's body while she placed soft kisses along her jawline.

Savannah pressed her eyes shut and tried to focus on the feeling.

It felt good. Fantastic even. But still, she felt her eyes get teary.

She wanted to tell her to stop. Wanted to tell her to wait. That it was a mistake.

The truth was, Savannah felt depressed.

Some days were okay, and some days were not so okay. Some days she just wanted to disappear. Of course, everything had become better since Bethany was back in her life; of course, she gave her so much strength every day. But as hard as she tried to fight the feeling, the sadness and self-hatred often washed over her, and there was nothing she could do about it.

Sometimes she felt like shaking Bethany, felt like telling her to pack her things and leave before it was too late.

*Look at me. I have nothing to offer you!* she wanted to tell her. *What do you want here? Go and live your life, Beth. Go and be with someone great. Go before I get weaker. Go before you see me lying in bed connected to machines. Before I'm too weak to eat—to talk. Just go!*

In her head, she had so often yelled these words at her. But she also knew her head was screwing with her. She knew in her heart she wanted Bethany more than anything in this world. She knew she wanted to finish the bucket list with her. But some days, her body betrayed her.

She had tried to get up, tried to move on to another item on the list, but her body wouldn't let her. It felt like being paralyzed. As if her head and body were no longer willing to cooperate. As if all she could do was stay in bed forever.

And Bethany had been so patient with her in these past weeks. She had tried to talk to her about her feelings, and when that hadn't worked, she had tried to distract her. With silly things. With funny anecdotes. With movies. With freshly baked cookies. With everything she had.

At least they had managed to paint their front door red the other day. Savannah had felt a little bit better, and they had bought the shiny, red color together before dressing up in old, white clothes and arming themselves with two extra-huge paint brushes.

Bethany had folded them two big hats out of old newspapers. They had looked ridiculous but, Savannah had to admit, also ridiculously cute.

Of course the paint had ended up all over their clothes, their faces, their hair, and the hallway.

Mrs. McPherson had completely freaked out, had told them she'd call the landlord, but somehow Bethany had managed to calm her down. It was something she was really good at, calming other people down.

They had giggled a lot, had kissed each other with red-painted noses until Bethany had suggested showering together. And Savannah's smile had frozen on her lips.

Bethany didn't ask again.

Savannah was fisting the sheets now, trying to control her heartbeat and her emotions while Bethany was kissing her way up to her earlobe and softly caressed the skin with her tongue.

It was fucking unfair.

She was twenty-five years old. She wanted to shower with her girlfriend, wanted to sleep with her and enjoy it. Wanted this suffocating fear to go away. Wanted to live.

"Are you okay?" Bethany whispered.

"I'm so sorry," Savannah replied. Looking at Bethany's sad blue eyes hurt in her chest.

Bethany tried to smile and softly brushed some strands of brown hair out of Savannah's face, behind her ear. She kissed her nose as her thumb lightly stroked along Savannah's chin.

"It's all right. Everything's fine, okay? I promise."

Nothing was all right. Nothing was fine. And they both knew it. But it was still good to hear Bethany say it.

Savannah nodded before Bethany's lips found hers again. Just one kiss, telling her, "I'm here for you." It was enough.

"I'm going to take a shower, okay?" Bethany asked. "And I have to run some errands soon."

Savannah swallowed and nodded. She hated the thick lump in her throat.

Bethany got up, and suddenly the bed was empty and cold.

She wanted to tell her to come back. Wanted to tell her not to leave. To stay with her. To kiss her. To touch her. To make her forget about everything. To get her heart to slow down. But no words came out of her mouth.

Savannah closed her eyes again when she finally heard the water running in the shower.

Bethany was waiting in front of the white door, her hand resting quietly against the wood panelling. She swallowed, not sure whether to knock or just leave.

She felt a shiver run through her body, even though the building was heated and her coat was supposed to keep her warm. It was one of those fast shivers that started at the back of your neck and quickly shot through your spine, all the way down to your feet.

Then she knocked.

"Come in!" she heard the friendly voice from inside and slowly opened the door, still a little hesitant.

When she stepped inside, she could see the surprised look on Loredana's face.

"Bethany?" she asked and got up from her seat. "Everything okay? Is Savannah—"

"Savannah is all right," Bethany assured her and silently closed the door.

"Okay, good." Loredana smiled and motioned Bethany to take a seat.

"How can I help you?"

Bethany tried not to be overwhelmed by the memories from her last visit and took a deep breath.

"It's about Savannah, obviously." She toyed with the scarf around her neck. "I wanted to ask you something."

"What is it?" Loredana asked.

"Okay. So…" she stuttered. "Savannah and I, we're doing this, well, *thing*. We're kinda trying to do a lot of things like, you know, things she wants to do before…"

Loredana nodded.

"Savannah wants to see Paris," Bethany blurted out. "But I don't want to take her to Europe if… I wanted to check with you first. I don't want to take her there if you think that…" She sighed. "Do you think it's too much for her?"

Loredana smiled.

"I see," she answered thoughtfully. "To be honest, Bethany, I'm not sure if it's a good idea. You know, this would be quite a big trip, and while I think that Savannah's been remarkably strong lately, I do think that a trip to another continent might come with a few risks. I'm not going to lie. I think that, in her condition, it might be safer to stay in this country."

Bethany swallowed.

"I know there are good doctors everywhere," she continued, "but it might get complicated. It might be better for her to stay as close to her own doctors as possible. I think you should consider it very carefully. It'd be a long flight, and most likely a lot of stress."

"It's okay," Bethany interrupted her. "I understand. That's why I came here. I was afraid you'd say that." She looked down at her hands, which were shaking slightly, and bit the inside of her cheek. She had expected it. The doctor was right. She had to accept this, as sad as it was.

Loredana reached over the table to take Bethany's hand. "I think it's remarkable that you want to do this for her. I think it's amazing what you two have and what a great support you are for her."

"Yeah." Bethany breathed out. "But it doesn't change anything. I mean, there's nothing I can do to make her better."

"That's not true," Loredana told her and shook her head. "You've already done more than you can imagine. I mean, the latest test results were really good."

*Good? Good results?*

"They were?" Bethany asked, barely able to hold back her excitement. "She's getting better? Tell me she's getting better!"

She knew Savannah was still in pain quite often. She was often tired, often weak, but maybe the medication really did its work. Maybe the doctors would change their mind. Maybe she could really try another chemo. Maybe it was that green tea. She had made sure that Savannah drank it every night before sleep.

Loredana closed her eyes for a second before continuing.

"No. I mean… That's not what I meant."

*Of course not.*

"Bethany. Savannah isn't going to get better, but she's not getting worse at the moment."

"This is not exactly what I was hoping to hear now," Bethany answered slowly.

"I know. But listen to me," Loredana said, her voice calm and friendly. "It's already a small miracle." She smiled.

"You know, when Savannah was first diagnosed and then when the chemo didn't do its work, honestly I expected her to have only a few more months left."

Bethany stared at her, trying to stay calm.

"I expected her condition to get worse quickly, because the cancer had already spread that far. And even though I'm still young, I've seen a lot of different patients in my career, a lot of patients with very similar conditions. And believe me when I say this, Savannah's strength is amazing. It's remarkable."

It was good to hear her say these words, but it also hurt so much.

"And seriously, since you've come back into her life…" Loredana said, squeezing Bethany's hand. "Since you're back, it's as if you're giving her even more strength. It's as if her body is fighting this cancer with every fiber. Things could be a lot worse at this point. But the way it looks right now, I am fairly certain that you will still have time with her. I mean, considering the circumstances. More time than I ever thought possible."

Despite all her efforts to numb her emotions for the visit, Bethany, of course, couldn't keep the tears from welling up.

"You can be so proud of what you two have and what it's doing for her."

Bethany brushed away the tears with her sleeve and shook her head. "But I don't feel as if I can truly help her lately, I don't. I mean, she's so sad. Sometimes it's okay, but then, like, she just sits there and stares. She doesn't want to get up. She doesn't want me to touch her."

She made a fist in her pocket. She didn't want to cry in front of Loredana again, for God's sake. "I'm sorry. This is probably too much information," Bethany quickly added.

"Hey, no, it's all right." Loredana was still stroking Bethany's hand reassuringly. "But Bethany, trust me. This is normal. I know that Savannah loves you more than anything. I mean, I've never had such a close relationship with any of my patients, and it's more appropriate to keep a professional distance, but I'm telling you this as a friend and not as her doctor, okay? Savannah always wanted to be with you, and all this strength she's showing, it's the strength she's getting from her love for you."

Bethany nodded. *Stupid tears. Go away.*

"Fear and depression are very common side effects of cancer," Loredana stated. "When she heard the diagnosis for the first time and then when she ended things with you, believe me, Savannah was a mess. She talked to a therapist, and she learned to cope with it, but it was hard. She was so close to giving up so often. But it's not like that anymore. I've seen the changes in her."

"I just want her to be happy," Bethany told her. Her voice was shaking.

"I know that. But you have to try to understand that it has nothing to do with you. She's as happy as you can possibly make her. But she's scared. Even if she doesn't want to admit it," Loredana explained. "Death is a scary topic. Nobody knows what happens after, you know? Nobody knows when it's going to happen. She's scared of leaving you. Scared of how you're going to deal with it."

"But she shouldn't worry about me. She should focus on herself."

"Of course she's worried about you, Bethany," Loredana continued, smiling softly. "That's why it's important that you two are totally honest with each other. That you talk about what you're afraid of. That you talk about the future."

"Yeah. Yeah, I guess." Bethany nodded.

"And," Loredana cleared her throat, "about the touching. About being close to her…"

"Mm?"

"I know it's hard, but keep trying to make her feel comfortable with herself. Many cancer patients experience this, and it's hard for both the patient and their partner. The medication is one part of it; lack of sexual desire can be a common side effect. But then there's the other side, the changes in the patient's body. Many people who've been through chemo and experience losing their hair, losing weight, occasionally losing control over their own body, they have a very different picture of themselves than they've had before. Even if you probably still see Savannah as the beautiful woman she's always been, it is not the same for her."

Bethany shook her head. "She's the most beautiful person I know," she stated honestly. She couldn't stand the thought of Savannah feeling that insecure about herself. She wanted to run home and tell her that. That looking at her still made her knees weak. That she had never desired anyone as much as she desired her.

"I believe you mean that," Loredana said. "And she's going to believe you too. Just give her some time. Just try to show her what you truly feel, and I'm sure she will be able to trust you enough to let you come a little closer again."

It was hard to take, this journey into Savannah's head. And as comforting as Loredana's words were, all Bethany wanted to do was take the pain away from Savannah. Because right now? Right now it was as if she could feel every bit of that pain in her own body and her own heart.

"Thank you," she whispered, not knowing what else to say. "Thanks so much for talking to me."

"Anytime," Loredana assured her. "Really, whenever you or Savy need advice, you know where to find me."

"Yes. Yes, thank you." Bethany got up from her chair, and Loredana quickly followed her example.

Loredana held out her hand for Bethany to shake it, but Bethany quickly wrapped her arms around her to press her close against her body. She didn't care that this was almost a stranger. She needed this right now.

She took a deep breath when the door to the doctor's office closed behind her.

What was she supposed to do now? Savannah wanted a kiss in front of the Eiffel Tower, and she was going to get a kiss in front of the Eiffel Tower. She'd find a way.

Her mind was working hard, and she went through all possible scenarios when suddenly she had an idea.

*Yeah. This might work.*

Bethany grabbed her bag to search for her phone. She turned it on, then opened her Facebook app.

She knew what she wanted to do, but Bethany also knew she could use some help.

Savannah still hadn't moved. She was still lying in bed. She had fallen asleep, had woken up after a few hours just to find that Bethany still hadn't returned, then had fallen asleep again.

It was late afternoon by now, and she was starting to get worried. This was odd.

Bethany often left the house when Savannah felt like staying inside, but usually she came back after a short time once she had shopped for a few groceries or had run some other errands.

How long had she been gone now? Seven hours? Eight?

Had she scared her away? Did she need space? Was it getting to be too much for her?

Savannah buried her face in her pillow. This was just fucking perfect. She had dragged Bethany down with her, hadn't she? All because she couldn't move her fucking ass out of bed. Because she was so fucking unmotivated. Because she hadn't shown any interest in any other bucket-list bullet points. Because she sucked. Fuck this.

She dragged the blanket over her head and was sweating under the warm material. She didn't care about the lack of oxygen; she just wanted to shut out the world. She'd just wait in her little cave until Bethany returned. She'd try to apologize.

*If* Bethany returned.

Savannah was so caught up in her own anger with herself that she hadn't noticed Bethany coming back inside and storming into the bedroom.

"Sorry I've been gone so long, but now it's time for you to get up!" she almost yelled as she ripped the curtains open and let the late-afternoon sunlight stream into the room.

Bethany's unexpected voice almost gave Savannah a heart attack, and she carefully peeked out from under her blanket. She frowned as she saw Bethany opening a suitcase and throwing all kinds of different clothes inside.

"What on earth are you doing?" she asked, her eyes trying to follow Bethany's quick movements.

"Honey, you need to shower. We're leaving. I know you want to protest, but you're gonna like this."

Savannah shook her head, the blanket still pulled all the way up to her chin.

Bethany dropped the dress in her hand. Then she smiled and hopped onto the mattress next to her.

"Savy," she started and slowly crawled underneath the blanket herself. She kissed Savannah's cheek and took her hand in hers.

"You've spent enough time in Snuggleland," she told her. "I like it too, and I absolutely want to come back here, but right now, I have a surprise for you."

Savannah had to smile a little at Bethany, whose fingers were pulling her close and whose grin was so big it was contagious.

"Bethany Sophia Peters, you've had too many surprises for me in these past weeks," she told her before Bethany's lips found her own and her eyes shut, instinctively.

"And you liked all of them, didn't you?" Bethany mumbled, her mouth still pressed against Savannah's.

Savannah smirked. *Yeah, damn it. Of course I liked them.*

She nodded. "Okay, okay. I'm getting up."

"Perfect!" Bethany squealed and quickly threw the blanket off of the bed. She hopped off the mattress again and helped Savannah get up.

Savannah sighed, accepted the hand, and was gently pulled out of bed.

"You look beautiful today," Bethany whispered, and Savannah couldn't deny that it felt good to hear her say it. "But now go shower. I will take care of the rest!"

Bethany gave her a playful slap on her butt as she pushed Savannah into the bathroom. Savannah chuckled and shook her head.

*How does she do it? How does she always make the impossible possible? How does she manage to make me feel as if all the sadness were just an unnecessary waste of time?*

Savannah took her time in the shower. She tried to enjoy the water on her skin and to wash away the dark thoughts. She took in the smell of Bethany's shampoo, which was filling the bathroom, and let the soft foam run down her body. She watched it disappear down the drain, hoping it would take all the bad feelings with it.

When Savannah finally came out of the bathroom, Bethany had finished packing and was looking at some stuff in her purse. Savannah smiled at her and just then realized that, for the first time since they had gotten back together, she hadn't gotten dressed before coming out.

"You look stunning," Bethany said with complete sincerity, and as hard as it was, Savannah believed her. They were standing like that for a moment, just looking at each other, when the sound of a car honking woke them from their little trance.

"That is our cab," Bethany said, grinning. "You better put on some clothes!"

"How long are we gonna be gone?"

Bethany winked at her.

"Just for a day. We'll be back tomorrow night."

Savannah decided not to ask any more questions for now.

When she had finally put her shoes and jacket on, they left the apartment, and Bethany locked the door behind them.

It was already dark outside. A cool winter night. The sky was clear, and the cab was waiting for them in the driveway.

"I really want to know where we're going," Savannah said as she opened the back door, freezing as she looked inside.

"Get inside!" a cheerful voice told her, and Savannah thought her heart must have stopped. "We're going to Vegas!"

The voice belonged to Joan Foster, Bethany's and Savannah's best high school friend.

Savannah still couldn't believe what was happening when the plane had almost landed four hours later. She couldn't believe Bethany had managed to arrange a last-minute flight. She couldn't believe she had contacted Joan and that Joan had been spontaneous enough to do this with them.

She had felt entirely insecure at first, not knowing what to say, not knowing what Joan knew about her. But her friend had made it very easy for her.

Joan had talked nonstop, had told her that she'd wanted to call them so many times in the past years but never had the guts to do it after their unnecessary fight ages ago. She told her that she was proud to have finished her studies but that she was in between jobs now and visiting her mother for a few weeks. That she had been in a relationship with some church guy who had been driving her crazy in the end. That Bethany's message had been like a sign, like a small relief she had been waiting for all this time, the perfect chance to let loose a little and clear her head. She said how good it was to see them again.

Savannah laughed a lot, and it was as if nothing had changed. Joan was still Joan, even if she seemed more mature and a lot more confident about herself.

"By the way, I love the new haircut. It really suits you," Joan told her as she was looking out of the window, watching the plane move closer to the earth again.

"Thanks," Savannah replied and glanced over to Bethany, who was holding her hand, smiling.

"This is gonna be so much fun!" Bethany exclaimed happily and let her head rest on Savannah's shoulder.

"Absolutely," Joan grinned. "Never been here. Always wanted to go."

Being surrounded by her two favourite blondes made Savannah's stomach tingle with excitement.

*Vegas.*

She hadn't actually thought of going here before. Why hadn't she? She totally should have put it on the list herself.

They didn't have to waste any time on waiting for their luggage as they had only brought cabin bags.

"I don't even know what I want to see first!" Bethany twittered, barely able to keep her feet still. "There must be so many good shows. And I'm hungry. I want to eat. And dance! I want to dance. Can we dance?"

Savannah chuckled. "I guess we should try to do as much as possible. I slept all day. I'm full of energy."

They stood in front of the airport and looked around. Joan was keeping her eyes open as well and scanning the area.

"Should we take a bus or something?" Savannah asked, but Joan and Bethany just looked at each other with a knowing grin.

"A bus? Are you kidding?" Joan laughed. "We're classier than that."

When Savannah spotted the black stretch limousine, she immediately understood what her friends had been up to.

"Oh God… How?" She shook her head in disbelief.

"I have connections," Joan replied with a wink.

Savannah couldn't believe she would have spent tonight in bed. Now she was in Vegas, and a friendly chauffeur in a black uniform and hat greeted her.

"Ladies," he said, holding the door open. "There's champagne and there are snacks. Just make yourself comfortable and enjoy the ride."

*Holy hell, this must have cost them a fortune.*

For a second, Savannah wanted to worry about Bethany's money, wanted to worry about the fact that her friend seemed to be spending all of her savings to make her happy, but then she looked at her. Saw her face. Saw her smile. Her excitement. And somehow she knew. This wasn't only about making *her* happy, it was about them being happy together.

Joan opened the cork of the bottle with a loud popping sound, and some of the sparkling liquid was running down her fingers. She grinned. "Girls, your glasses, please!"

Savannah knew that getting drunk wasn't the wisest decision, but she was going to allow herself one drink.

"Cheers! To a fabulous night!" Joan exclaimed, and they clonked their glasses together.

Savannah enjoyed the warm feeling of the bubbly in her stomach and didn't hesitate to give Bethany a long and passionate kiss.

"You two still can't keep your hands off of each other," Joan smirked and took a sip herself.

"Oh. We've…we've actually been broken up for a year and only recently got back together," Bethany explained before smiling shyly.

"I'm glad you did," Joan told them honestly. "You two belong together. You always have."

Savannah smiled. "Yeah, I guess we have."

All of them were enjoying the tour, so they opened the window above their heads.

Savannah was the first to get up and look outside. She was completely overwhelmed by all the colorful lights and the energy surrounding her. Everything was full of people, full of laughter, full of music.

The shadows of the shining buildings fell across her face, and she closed her eyes for a moment to take in the breeze on her face and the different smells and sounds. It was better than anything she had imagined before. Maybe it was Beth's presence that made it so good.

"So? What hotel are we staying at?" Savannah asked when she climbed back onto her seat, her cheeks rosy.

Bethany's smile brightened. "What do you think?" she told her, biting her lower lip, grinning. "The Paris Hotel."

All the impressions had been almost too much to process. It was late, but Vegas was wide awake.

They had managed to get tickets for the Cirque de Soleil show, and Savannah didn't know what had been better—watching those talented artists fly through the air or listening to Bethany's constant "oohs" and "aahs." She figured it was the combination of both.

Bethany was getting a little tipsy, and Joan and Savannah snickered several times, because Bethany wasn't able to shut up. She blabbered happily and dragged them from one bar to the next.

They had tried to play a few slot machines at the casino, but in the end, they had left more money at the place than they had earned.

It didn't matter. As cheesy as it was, Savannah already felt lucky enough. At least tonight.

When they were finally in a club with a big dance floor, Bethany's excitement increased. It had been so long since Savannah had seen her dance. Too long. She said she had missed it.

She had to admit that she was beginning to feel exhausted, but she was doing her best to keep her strength. She watched Bethany dance with Joan, watched them laugh, and enjoyed the feeling of the loud bass in her veins.

Bethany looked stunning, and as tipsy as she was, it was fascinating how much control she had over her body and how she became one with the music as she sexily moved over the dance floor without any effort.

She felt Bethany's hands on her hips, felt her press her body against her from behind as their hips moved in unison.

"You're so sexy," Bethany breathed into her ear, and Savannah felt herself blush. Bethany had called her sexy a million times, but it had been a while.

"I've seen people stare at you," she continued as her hands were running up and down the side of her body. "I don't like it, but it also makes me proud, 'cause you're here with me. 'Cause you're dancing with me."

Savannah shook her head. "I don't think anyone's staring, Beth. If anything, they are looking at you, because you're pretty damn flawless."

"Uh-uh!" Bethany exclaimed. She turned Savannah around so she was facing her and held her close as they danced.

"See that chick over there? Earlier, when I was getting another drink, I heard her talk about you. She said you were hot. She was thinking about coming over to you and asking you to dance."

Savannah frowned. "You're making that up."

"I wish," Bethany told her before kissing her cheek and letting her hands disappear in the back pockets of her Savannah's pants. "But I told her you're here with me, and you know what?"

"What?" Savannah swallowed.

"You can't see it, but she's looking right at us, frustrated that I get to touch your cute butt."

"Beth!" Savannah exclaimed, rolling her eyes, but Bethany started giggling.

"I'm sorry, I think I had a bit too much of that bubbly. But I'm not lying."

Savannah shook her head again, but she grinned.

They danced like this for a little while longer while Joan was busy trying to tell some guy that she wasn't going to give him her number.

As much as Savannah wanted to dance with Bethany all night, she knew she had to sit down and have some water if she didn't want to let the weakness wash over her.

"Beth, I need a break." She got up on her tiptoes to kiss her forehead. "But please, keep dancing. I'm just going to sit down over there and get a drink."

Bethany looked concerned. "Are you sure? I can totally sit down with you."

"I'm sure. No worries. I'm going to help Joan get rid of the weird douche over there. I'm sure she'll be thankful," Savannah explained with a wink.

"Hm...okay," Bethany finally agreed and placed a quick kiss on Savannah's lips. "But tell me if you want to leave, we can leave whenever you need to."

"I'm good," Savannah promised with a smile.

She walked over to Joan and placed a hand on her hip as she looked at the grinning guy in front of her. "Sorry, man, she's here with me, and it's time for you to leave."

The guy was trying to protest, but Savannah hushed him by putting her finger on his lips. "Nuh-uh. Don't try to argue, Potato-Face, and don't even think about asking if you can join us."

Joan laughed when the man disappeared with a disappointed look on his face. "Thank you!" she exclaimed in relief.

"You're welcome." Savannah grinned and sat down on the barstool next to her friend.

Savannah could feel Joan's eyes on her, could see her smile from the corner of her eye.

"You having a good time?" Joan asked her when Savannah had ordered her water.

"Totally. It's the best night ever."

"I agree," Joan said. "I'm glad you're enjoying it. And so glad you let me come with you."

Savannah took a sip from the cold water, her eyes fixed on the dance floor. On Bethany. It was always a pleasure to watch her, even from a distance.

And it was surprising how much she enjoyed being here with Joan. It felt as if she could still trust her. She had always trusted Joan, even if they had almost ripped each other's hair out during some fights in their teenage years.

Savannah found herself overwhelmed with the sudden need to talk. With the sudden need to tell her everything. With the desire to get so many things off of her chest.

The three of them were great together. Even after all this time. She felt her body getting hotter. It made her nervous. The music was loud, and it was cheerful, but it felt as if time had stopped for a moment. As if things around her were happening in slow motion and it were only Joan and her in the room. Her heart was pounding in her chest.

"Joan," she started and swallowed hard.

"Savy?" Joan replied, her features more serious. As if she had noticed the switch in Savannah's mood right away.

"I think...I think I need to tell you something," Savannah continued. "I think you should know what this trip is about."

Joan looked down at her drink to stare at the bubbling liquid. Savannah could see her take a deep breath. "I know what it's about, Savy."

Savannah was gripping her glass a little harder. *Seriously? She told her?*

"But?" She stopped, clearing her throat. "You didn't say anything. You didn't act like you knew?"

Joan turned around in her chair to face Savannah. Her eyes looked sad all of a sudden, and keeping her gaze felt like a challenge.

"Would you have wanted to talk about it?" she asked her. "We're having an amazing night, Savy. It's the best night I've had in a very long time. And it isn't about anyone being sick. It isn't about fulfilling any wishes on some list you and Bethany made. It's just about the three of us. Just about three old friends having the time of their lives."

Savannah felt her cheeks turn hot. She wanted to cry.

"You're still the same Savannah I knew and loved back in high school. Nothing has changed, and nothing is going to change it. And if you want to talk about it, then I'm here. I'll always be here."

She bit the inside of her cheek in order not to lose it in the middle of this club. She tried to focus on the dance floor again and searched for Bethany in the crowd. Bethany was still enjoying her night, still lost in the sound of music.

She didn't dare look at Joan again, and she could see that Joan was doing the same, facing the dancers.

"Joan?"

"Hm?"

Savannah closed her eyes for a second. Her fingernails were digging into her flesh as she made a fist.

"Will you..." she swallowed, "will you look after her when I'm gone?"

They both kept looking at the ditzy blonde in front of them. At her careless smile. The happiness on her features.

"Of course I will."

Savannah didn't need to look at Joan to know that she was crying. "I promise you I'll be there for her. She won't be alone. I promise, Savannah."

It made Savannah think her heart might be about to explode. "Thank you," she whispered.

She didn't know if Joan could hear her words over the music, but when Joan's hand ended up on her thigh, squeezing it, she took Joan's hand in hers and knew it would be okay.

She knew Bethany was going to be okay.

All three of them were tired when they finally made it to their hotel.

"Here we are," Joan said and pointed at the huge building. It wasn't hard to recognize, considering they were looking at a big Eiffel Tower.

Sure, it wasn't as big as the real one, but it came pretty close.

"It looks amazing," Savannah admitted.

Bethany was already digging for the Polaroid. "Will you take a picture of us?" she asked Joan, not waiting for a reply as she pressed the camera against her friend's chest.

"Of course," Joan smiled.

Bethany looked at Savannah, took her hand and led her over to the tower.

"I'm sorry it's not really Paris," she whispered.

"Beth, it's better than that. It's perfect."

Bethany smiled, relieved.

"Okay, you two," Joan announced. "Smile for the camera. Wait, no. Kiss for the camera!" She winked.

Savannah took in the sight of Bethany in those beautiful surroundings, then looked over to Joan, who was waiting to snap the picture.

Another point on the list.

Another step closer to finishing the list.

Life could be beautiful. Yeah. Sometimes she wished she didn't have to leave. Sometimes it was worth it to leave her bed. She was glad she had people in her life to remind her of that.

"Come on, kiss me," Bethany whispered, and Savannah didn't need any more encouragement than that.

She wrapped her arms around Beth and closed her eyes when their lips touched.

Tonight, all three of them would sleep together in the same room, and they would wake up together in a new morning.

She kissed Bethany with everything she had, willing to enjoy every one of their kisses, willing to appreciate every waking minute with her.

And she didn't stop. She kissed her until she felt Joan tapping her shoulder.

"You can stop now. I have the picture. In fact, I already had it five minutes ago." She rolled her eyes. Savannah didn't reply. She just turned around to wrap her arms around Joan.

They stood there for a moment, hugging, until they felt another pair of arms around them and Bethany's blonde hair tickling their faces.

"I really like Paris," Bethany mumbled, and Savannah smiled as she heard Joan laugh next to her.

"Me too."

6. Paint my front door red—check.

7. Ride in a stretch limo and drink fancy champagne—check.

8. Have a girls night out with the Trashy Triplets—check.

9. Kiss in front of the Eiffel Tower—check.

# Chapter 11

It was the twenty-fourth of December, and Bethany woke up with a smile on her face. She loved Christmas. And she loved Christmas with Savannah.

The year before, she had spent the holidays alone with her mom, still heartbroken because of her breakup with Savannah. Of course, the circumstances this year weren't perfect either, and Bethany was aware that this might be the last Christmas she and Savannah would spend together—still, she wouldn't let this ruin her mood. She was going to make sure that they had a great time and would be able to enjoy the Christmas spirit to its fullest.

It was a Monday, and Bethany placed a quick kiss on Savannah's forehead before jumping out of bed and getting ready. She was waiting for one particular Amazon delivery—their Christmas tree.

While she waited for the parcel service, Bethany started preparing breakfast and texted with Joan. Their friend had gone back to New Haven about a week ago, but she had promised to come visit as often as possible. The three of them had spent a few more days together after their trip to Vegas, and already now Bethany was missing her. She was more than happy to have Joan back in their lives, and she knew Savannah felt the same way.

She put on some cheerful Christmas music and nibbled on one of the snowman-shaped cookies Savannah and she had baked together the previous night. Then the doorbell finally rang.

The packet was huge and rather heavy, and Bethany had trouble carrying the thing upstairs. When she finally managed to free the tree from its cardboard and Styrofoam, she looked at the pink branches with a satisfied smile on her face.

"I see we have a tree," Savannah said as she came into the living room and wiped some last bits of sleep out of her tired eyes.

"It looks awesome, Savy!" Bethany chirped happily and quickly placed a good-morning kiss on Savannah's lips. "Want to help me decorate it?"

"Do you even have to ask?" Savannah replied, grinning, before quickly searching for the box with tree decorations.

*Beth-Beth and Savannah's X-mas Stash* was written on it in crayon with a few colorful drawings next to it. It made Savannah smirk.

They put the tree in the middle of their living room and started wrapping garlands and different strings of Christmas lights around the branches. Already the tree looked chaotic, considering that most colors didn't go too well with pink, but they didn't care. It was their tree, and to them, it looked more than charming.

Bethany was wearing a reindeer sweater and was pleased that Savannah had put on a pullover with red and white stripes. Savannah had never been a big fan of Christmas outfits, but this year, Bethany didn't even have to ask her to do it.

When "All I Want for Christmas Is You" started playing on the stereo, Savannah sang along, and Bethany felt all warm inside. It had been so long since she had last heard Savannah sing, and she had missed the sound of her beautiful voice. At some point, Bethany stopped decorating and just sat there on the floor, hugging her knees in front of her chest to listen to her. Only when she started looking in the box for some more Christmas tree baubles did Savannah seem to notice Bethany's gaze fixed on her. She blushed.

"Hey, you getting lazy?" Savannah asked, smiling shyly.

"Don't stop singing," Bethany replied. "It's beautiful."

"Err. Thanks," Savannah mumbled, and Bethany quickly joined the chorus to avoid any potential awkwardness.

"Can we put the Christmas duck on top?" she asked with a grin, and Savannah nodded.

"Of course."

When the box was empty, the two of them stared at the result in all its shining glory. Pink, purple, blue, yellow, red. A real rainbow tree. Bethany loved it.

"Should we put the presents underneath?" Savannah asked, and Bethany bit her lower lip.

"Um. Actually, I can't."

"Oh, I see; you didn't get me anything," Savannah teased.

"Of course I did! But I can't put it there. Not yet."

"Fair enough," Savannah shrugged. "Mine isn't exactly shaped like a real gift either." With that, she disappeared into the bedroom and returned with an envelope wrapped in a huge red bow. She put it under the tree anyway and stepped next to Bethany to take her hand in her own.

"We're going to have a great holiday," Savannah said, and Bethany squeezed her hand.

Savannah felt nervous as they stood in front of the Peterses' house, waiting for Bethany's mother to open the door.

Her father was, as was so often the case, on a business trip in Bangkok. Savannah knew Bethany hated it when he was gone over the holidays. Thankfully, the first few snowflakes had started falling earlier that day, so at least Bethany was happy about possibly building a snow woman with Savannah later that night.

When the door finally swung open, Savannah tried her best not to tear up. She loved Eliza Peters almost as much as Eliza loved her daughter. The woman had always treated Savannah as if she were part of the family, and she had spent countless nights at their place when they were younger. Savannah hadn't seen her in over a year, yet Eliza was looking at her with so much warmth in her eyes, she felt relieved. It was like coming home.

"Savannah. God, it's so good to see you. C'mere!" Eliza exclaimed and happily wrapped her arms around Savanah.

"It's good to see you too," Savannah smiled.

"Oh Lord, you're making an old woman cry. Let me just say—I was so mad at you and Bethany for breaking up, because it meant I didn't get to see you anymore," Eliza blathered. She was squeezing Savannah a little harder than necessary. "I made your favourite casserole. You still like my casserole, don't you? I left out the garlic, so you and Bethany can still kiss and—"

"Thank you!" Savannah interrupted the older woman before she could take the explanation any further. "I've been craving that casserole for months, Liz."

"Perfect," Eliza replied before ruffling Savannah's hair. "Love the new style. Let's go inside. Hi, sweetheart!"

"Hi, Mom!" Bethany gave Eliza a peck on her cheek.

The room already smelled like food, and Bing Crosby's voice was filling the air with some classic Christmas tunes. The table was set, candles were lit, and presents were wrapped. Just as in the good old times.

Eliza was filling each of their glasses with a little red wine before disappearing into the kitchen to get the food out of the oven.

Savannah smiled at Bethany and took a sip of her drink as she heard the first few words of *Have Yourself a Merry Little Christmas* playing on the stereo. By far her favourite song.

She wished she had appreciated these holidays a little more when she had still had the chance. She wished she had made the past years more magical for both of them. Now she was running out of time.

Savannah swallowed. What had she done last year? What had she been thinking?

She had been lying on her couch and watched *Mission Impossible* on DVD without really paying attention to it. There had been no decorations; there had been no food. She had been bitter.

At some point in the late evening, her phone had rung, her mother's name on the display. Christmas and her birthday had been the only days Gloria had tried to call her since their big fight, but Savannah had never had the strength to pick up. Especially not after getting her diagnosis. The topic had been done for her, once and for all, but now things were different.

She had come back to life, had given herself another chance at happiness.

And she was looking at Bethany's mother, watching her hug her daughter, watching them giggle. And as much as she loved both of them, she missed her own family.

"Sweetheart, what's on your mind?" Eliza asked when she realized that Savannah hadn't touched her casserole.

"Nothing," Savannah started, picking with her fork at the food. "It's just that I'm truly happy to be here, but..."

"You're missing your mom," Eliza finished for her as if it were the most obvious conclusion on earth.

"Yes. I mean, no. You've been like a mother to me, Liz," Savannah explained. "I just feel as if... I'm wondering if it's too late for me to make things right."

Bethany was squeezing her leg under the table while Eliza was shaking her head. "Savannah, let me tell you this from a mother's perspective." She put her own fork down and looked Savannah straight in the eye. "There is no point in time when a mother stops loving her own daughter. If I were in Gloria's position, the whole situation would be killing me. I know you both have said things that you regret and that were hurtful, but I know for sure that she thinks of you every day and hopes you will show up on her doorstep or give her a call."

Savannah's gaze dropped as she shook her head. "I don't know. I've hurt her. And how much is it going to hurt her to hear that..." She couldn't finish the sentence as the big lump in her throat made it hard to swallow.

Bethany was still stroking her thigh, and Savannah grabbed her hand under the table. She needed the touch for comfort.

"It's going to be rough for her, no doubt about that," Eliza started again and poured some more wine into everyone's glass. "But Savannah, she will find out, sooner or later. And in this case, sooner is definitely better than later. Look at me, sweetie."

Savannah swallowed before meeting Eliza's eyes again which were as teary as her own.

"Give her another chance. I'm not saying do it right now, I'm not even saying you should do it tomorrow or this week, but at least consider it. Give her a chance to make things right, to be a good mom to you for at least a little while longer. To hug you and comfort you. That's what moms are for, you know? We put our babies into this world for a reason, we want them to be all right. And even if we don't always agree with the choices they make or the things that they do—even if they drive us crazy sometimes—we want nothing more in the world than to be there for them and to know that we've done everything in our power to make them happy."

A tear rolled down her cheek, and Savannah blushed when she realized it. "It's just that in the past weeks, things have become so different. I think I've changed. Bethany changed me." Savannah looked at Bethany, smiling shyly. "Yeah, you did," she whispered. "I mean, I've accepted my disease. I've accepted what's going to happen. But somehow I can't accept the thought of leaving this place without having sorted out things with my family first."

"Savannah, that's good, but don't do it with the cancer in the back of your head. Don't let that be your only motivation," Eliza said slowly. "Do it because of your family and because you miss them. It's still your life, sweetie. It's not just a big to-do list of things that need to be handled. Do it because it's what you feel is right for you, and do it when you're ready. Don't pressure yourself. And we're both here for you; you know that."

Yeah, Savannah knew where Bethany got her big heart from. "Thank you."

Bethany was staring at the Christmas tree in front of them, then leaned over to kiss Savannah's cheek. Savannah had to smile at the gesture. She was glad to be cuddling up on the couch and ending Christmas Eve with just the two of them.

The way home had been nice. It had snowed a little more, and even if it wasn't enough to build a snow woman, it had still been enough to cover the streets in a pretty, sparkling white that looked amazing with all those beautiful Christmas decorations in their neighbourhood. Enough to cause that amazing creaking sound under their shoes as they walked. And enough to put a smile on Bethany's face.

She was reflecting on the evening and their time with Eliza, and it was so weird to think that her time was limited. That she wouldn't be having Christmas dinner at the table in the Peterses' dining room five or six years from now, maybe not even next year. That they would be living their lives without her. That she'd be nothing more than a memory.

Eliza would be a great grandmother—Savannah was sure of that. She would love to see her take care of their own child, spoil him or her with silly presents and teach the little Peters-Cortez some of her wise views on life and love. It hurt like hell to think about it, but Savannah truly hoped Bethany was going to have children one day, simply because the kid would be more than lucky to grow up around the two most lovable and kind-hearted women she knew.

And maybe they would tell the kid about her. That there was once this girl named Savannah Cortez and that she could be a bitch and a pain in the ass, but that they missed her. And that she would have loved to get to know them. Maybe they'd tell the little one some funny stories from when she and Beth were young. And maybe she'd still be a part of their lives, even if it was only sometimes, over dinner or during Scrabble nights.

She squeezed Bethany's hand a little harder.

Part of her hoped that being dead really meant simple darkness. That she'd just be gone. Because she didn't think she'd want her soul to be floating around in space, having to watch people live their lives. She'd miss Bethany too fucking much. Too much for words.

Savannah let her mind drift back to earlier in the evening.

*"So." Eliza cleared her throat. "I think I'm gonna put on my favorite rock Christmas sampler. What do you say?"*

*Bethany's mother was no fan of sadness or bad mood. And it was truly hard to stay sad around her.*

*"Beth, honey, will you go into the living room and push the furniture aside? I wanna dance to 'Run, Run, Rudolph' with my two favorite girls. Shake off those bad holiday calories."*

*"Sure!" Bethany replied before running over to her mother and whispering something into her ear that Savannah couldn't understand.*

*Eliza replied and gave her daughter a wink before laughing in Savannah's direction.*

Savannah ran her fingertips up and down Bethany's arm before softly nudging her shoulder.

"So what was that whispering about earlier?" she asked her, trying to sound casual and not as curious as she felt.

Bethany shifted nervously in her seat.

"Whispering?" she replied.

AC Oswald

"Oh come on, Beth. First you and your mom whisper and laugh, then Eliza starts distracting me with her joss stick collection, and then you disappear. By the way, did you know she has joss sticks that smell like weed? Just sayin'."

Bethany started giggling. "Okay, okay, you got me. Well..." she looked at her watch. "It's almost midnight, so we might as well start now."

"Start with what?" Savannah asked.

"I want to give you your present!" Bethany said, and Savannah laughed.

"Okay, then. I must say I'm a little curious."

"Gimme a sec!" Bethany chirped and ran out of the room.

Savannah waited patiently, then her eyes widened when she saw Bethany carry a medium-sized basket with a big bow into the room. She could see that her girlfriend was careful not to drop it.

"Merry Christmas, Savy," she whispered before putting the basket down between them.

Savannah looked inside and frowned before realizing what she was looking at.

"He's asleep," Bethany said, smiling, and Savannah felt her heart beat a little faster.

It was a tiny kitten, snoozing peacefully, wrapped in a fluffy red blanket. Its fur was light brown with some dark brown stripes. It looked almost like...

"I thought we could name him 'Tiger'!"

Savannah grinned. Yeah. A tiger.

"I think 'Tigger' might be more fitting, actually," she replied and carefully petted the small cat's head with her index finger.

"A real tiger was really hard to get," Bethany pouted. "I called a few different zoos, but all they offered me was a sponsorship for one of their old polar bears."

"I love him, Beth," Savannah whispered. "He's so small."

"He's only a few weeks old," Bethany said smiling. "He's going to be our baby."

Savannah nodded. "Thank you so much, Beth. Really."

"You're welcome, and I'm so happy you like him. Actually I've got the whole trunk full of equipment. Food, toys, a cat tree."

"He's going have a good life here," Savannah told her with a wink. "But now I still have something for you."

She got up to grab the envelope that was still lying under the tree. Her hand was shaking slightly as she handed it over to Bethany.

"Please tell me if you hate it. Really, be honest. It's okay if you don't want to, I mean."

"Savy!" Bethany interrupted her. "I haven't even opened it yet."

"Right. Sorry."

Bethany carefully unwrapped the bow and extracted a little piece of paper from the envelope which she slowly unfolded. She read what was written on it, and Savannah could see the emotions change on Bethany's features.

"Savy, that's… it's…"

"A coupon for a tattoo, yes." Savannah finished for her. "And I understand if you don't want to do it. I mean, you never said that you wanted a tattoo. I just thought it would connect us."

Savannah had spent a long time thinking about what she wanted her tattoo to look like. She knew it was about time that she took at least one point on the list into her own hands. Designing her own tattoo was the obvious choice.

But she didn't want anything too simple. She didn't just want something tribal or some ugly tramp stamp. She wanted it to mean something to her. And there was nothing in the world that meant more to her than Bethany.

She had thought about getting Bethany's first name tattooed on her chest, but then decided that this was silly and not very creative. A portrait? No. Definitely not; they usually turned out super creepy.

Then one afternoon, while Bethany had been out running errands, a new thought had hit her.

She didn't want a tattoo on her chest, nor on her arm. She wanted it to be on her pinky finger. And she wanted the other part to be on Bethany's.

She had taken a piece of paper and tried out a few phrases, a few different designs, but then decided to go for the most personal thing she could think of. Her own handwriting on Bethany's finger, and Bethany's handwriting on hers.

"What do you want the tattoo to say?" Bethany asked.

Savannah cleared her throat, her cheeks turning hot.

"I thought about, 'Love…' on my pinky and '…forever unbroken' on yours." She cleared her throat again. "Do you, um, like it? Please be honest."

"It's perfect, Savannah," Bethany whispered. "I'd be honored."

Savannah felt as if a heavy weight had just fallen off her chest, and she quickly wiped away some tears with the back of her sleeve.

"It's the most beautiful Christmas gift you've ever given me," Bethany added before wrapping her arms around Savannah.

"I love you," Savannah told her, and Bethany placed a kiss on her shoulder, mumbling, "I love you too."

Savannah carefully put the basket with a sleeping Tigger on the floor before looking at Bethany again. She was so beautiful, and somehow she felt silly for having been so distant in the past weeks. She could see it in her eyes, could see that the woman in front of her loved her more than anything in this world. She didn't know why she had been so insecure all this time.

Not once had Bethany acted weird around her or made her feel uncomfortable. In fact, she had done everything in her power to be there for her and make her smile every single day.

She didn't know what to say, how to express what she felt in this moment, so she just leaned over to kiss her once more and closed her eyes to enjoy the feeling of her girlfriend's lips against her own.

Bethany's lips parted right away, and Savannah deepened the kiss. Her hand was on Bethany's thigh and slowly started caressing it. Savannah could feel her heart beating faster in her chest. She was nervous about what was going to happen. All she knew was that she wanted to be close to her, wanted to touch her, wanted to feel Beth's skin against her own. She wasn't sure when she had felt it so strongly the last time, the need to be with her. The need to be one.

"I want to make love to you," she whispered against Bethany's lips. Then she cupped her cheek with her hand and let her thumb slowly run along her chin.

Bethany pulled away for a second and searched for something in Savy's eyes.

With a shy smile, Savannah nodded, and Bethany smiled back at her before grabbing the hem of her own shirt and pulling it over her head in one fluid movement.

Savannah bit her lower lip at the sight in front of her: Bethany in jeans and a purple bra, looking at her with flushed cheeks and pouty lips, chest heaving slightly.

She quickly got rid of her own shirt before moving closer and placing soft kisses along Bethany's cleavage. She took Bethany's hands in hers and entangled their fingers before letting her tongue run along her collarbone and licked every inch of soft porcelain skin.

Savannah pushed one purple strap off Bethany's shoulder, caressed the exposed skin with her lips, and slowly reached around to unclasp her bra.

The living room felt hot, but all Savannah could think was that she felt alive. Truly alive for the first time in months.

A soft moan escaped Bethany's mouth when Savannah's closed around one of her nipples, and Savannah could feel Bethany's hand on her neck as it grabbed a fistful of dark hair to urge her on. It felt as if nothing had changed. It still felt as if Bethany were her perfect counterpart. The way their bodies moved together so easily had always amazed her, and she knew she could let herself go. Completely.

Bethany was stroking Savannah's hair, smiling, as she herself opened Savannah's bra and pushed her softly against the sofa.

"You're so beautiful," Bethany whispered. "I love you so much."

If she had thought her heart had been beating fast before, it was nothing compared to the hammering in her chest as she noticed Bethany fumbling with the fly of her pants. She could feel her fingertips against her belly, and the excitement was driving her crazy.

"I've missed this," Savannah breathed out. "I hadn't realized how much I truly missed this."

Bethany smiled as she slowly opened the zipper and kissed her way down to Savannah's belly button. She left some soft kisses there and slowly pulled the jeans down her legs.

She kissed her way up again, caressing the inside of Savannah's thighs in the process before quickly removing her own pants and underwear. Her blonde hair was falling into her face as she carefully moved on top of Savannah, kissed her, and parted her legs with one of her thighs.

Their kisses had become more passionate, and Savannah couldn't wait to feel her finally. She took Bethany's hand and slowly led it down between her legs, not once breaking their gaze.

Bethany didn't need more encouragement than that; one of her fingers slowly disappeared into Savannah's panties.

"Oh," Savannah sighed as she pressed her eyes shut to focus on the feeling of her girlfriend's fingertip against her clit.

Bethany was stroking her softly, up and down, Savannah's extreme arousal making it easy for Bethany's finger to caress her most sensitive spot. It felt as if Savannah's whole body were on fire, all senses on overload. How long had it been? Too fucking long.

Savannah kissed her hungrily, bucking her hips, wishing she'd go a little faster, wishing she'd fill her up completely. Already her fingernails were digging into Bethany's back, and they had just started.

She figured Bethany could sense how impatient she was getting, as she finally pushed a finger inside, slowly, going deeper, inch by inch. Savannah held her close and pressed her body against Bethany's before dragging her head down to whisper into her ear. "Beth. Don't worry. I'm not gonna break."

If Bethany was holding back because she thought it might be too much for Savannah, then Savannah had to prove her wrong. She didn't feel tired or exhausted; part of her felt like her old self again, like the Savannah she had wanted to be but who had disappeared somewhere into a dark and bitter hole. But not now. Not tonight.

Bethany smiled and nodded before adding another finger and pushing it all the way in, a little faster, a little harder than before.

"Oh, yes. Yes. Like that."

Savannah soon started panting, eyes closed, as she focused on the amazing feeling of being as close to Bethany as possible. She wanted this moment to last forever. She pushed her own leg up, slowly rubbing it against Bethany's wet center as her eyes fluttered open again. She wanted to see her, wanted to see the look on her girlfriend's face as she moaned, the passionate sparkle in her pretty blue eyes as Savannah rubbed herself against her.

And Bethany did just that, finding her own rhythm as she started riding Savannah's leg, all the while still bringing Savannah closer to the edge with her fingers.

Bethany knew Savannah's body so well, even after all this time. She knew exactly how to satisfy her, knew exactly what would make her eyes roll back into her head.

"You're so hot. Fuck, I love you. I've missed you. Love you so much," she panted against Savannah's neck, her breath hot against her skin.

Her thumb was on Savannah's clit, her hips moving faster, her moans getting shorter.

Savannah had almost forgotten that this was the best part of having sex with Bethany—watching her getting close, watching her come undone. And the fact that she was the one who brought her there, that she was the cause of that pleasure, never ceased to amaze her.

"I'm so close. I'm gonna. I…"

"Me too," Savannah whispered, pulling Bethany in for another kiss. She pressed her lips on hers as hard as she could, muffling a deep groan as her own orgasm washed over her. Oh fuck. Why hadn't they done this sooner? Why?

It felt as if her body were leaving the sofa, every tiny muscle in her body tensing at once, mixed with this one particular indescribable feeling. And she was sharing it with the one person who meant everything to her. What could be better? Nothing. Absolutely nothing.

Bethany just lay on top of her for several minutes, trying to catch her breath, and Savannah enjoyed the feeling of the sweat slowly cooling her skin.

Why couldn't she just stop time? Why couldn't she just stay with her like this forever, her arms wrapped around Bethany's exhausted body, softly stroking her back, kissing her forehead, listening to her breathing?

Bethany raised her head to look at her and smiled, her eyes a little tired. She kissed her nose.

"That was amazing. So good. If I weren't so tired, I'd totally want to do it again."

Savannah laughed and kissed her once more. "I promise we'll do it again tomorrow morning. And tomorrow afternoon. And tomorrow night. And the day after tomorrow."

"I like the sound of that," Bethany said, smiling brightly. "But oh my God, now I'm so hungry. Do you mind if I warm up some of the leftovers in the microwave? Do you want some?"

"Let me fix it for you," Savannah suggested and quickly walked over to the kitchen. She didn't even think about putting on clothes anymore.

The loud 'ping' of the microwave indicated that the food was done. Savannah carried it back into the living room. She sat down next to Bethany, who smiled as her eyes ended up on their book. She opened it and grabbed a pen and crossed off more points on their list. She then stared at it, lost in thought.

What was putting that frown on Bethany's pretty forehead? "What's on your mind?" she asked.

"I want to ask you something," Bethany began carefully as she took the plate from Savannah and stuffed some of the casserole into her mouth. "Thanks, by the way."

"You're welcome. So…what's up?"

"The last point on the list. I honestly don't believe you when you say you don't remember what you wanted to say there."

"Beth," Savannah sighed. "Really, it's…it's nothing. Can't we just forget about it? We have enough points left that we can worry about."

Bethany shook her head, put the plate on the table, and came closer to Savannah.

"Honestly, Savy, if you don't want to tell me, may I add something to the list myself? I mean, it's Christmas, after all. Can I make a wish?"

Savannah frowned curiously. Yes, Bethany had managed to grant her so many wishes already, the least she could do was try to grant her one as well. But what did she want? "Yeah. Sure. Add whatever you'd like."

Something told Savannah that she wasn't going to wish for a baby duck or an elephant ride. Something told her that this was more serious, and she could feel herself getting nervous.

Bethany's pen touched the paper where the *B* was still written in Savannah's handwriting, and Savannah could see her swallow as she finished the point.

Then she looked up at her, searching her eyes expectantly.

*Be my wife* was written on the list, and Savannah's heart skipped a beat.

"What do you say?" Bethany whispered, her voice shaky.

Savannah didn't know how much time had passed until she found her voice again. She didn't know if she should tell her that this was exactly what she had wanted to write—*Being your wife*. She didn't know anything anymore.

"Hm?" Bethany tried again, nervously biting her lower lip.

"Beth, I don't know what to say."

"Say what's on your mind," Bethany told her, her arms crossed in front of her still-naked chest. "Do you want to marry me? Or would you rather not?"

"Beth, of course I want to marry you," Savannah said, her cheeks burning. "But...I can't expect this from you, I mean, it's too much. We won't have much time, we—"

"Savannah," Bethany interrupted her, her voice firm. "I love you. You're the love of my life."

She was looking into Savannah's eyes with pure honesty, the lights of the Christmas candles reflecting in her shining blue eyes. "I've loved you my whole life, and even when we were still young, I knew I wanted to marry you. It probably sounds stupid, but it's true." She visibly swallowed. "I want you to be my wife. I want to be your wife. We don't know how much time we still have, but nobody knows that. No one who gets married knows how much time they're going to have. One person could suddenly become sick, could get in an unexpected accident. They might get divorced. All I know is that I love you with everything I have, and when I look back at my life, I want to be able to say 'I married the woman of my dreams.' It's not about time, Savannah. It's about love. And I have a lot of that to offer."

Savannah's eyes were teary, yet she had to laugh. "Why are you so much smarter than me?" she asked Bethany and quickly brushed away a tear.

Bethany's smile brightened. "Is that a yes?"

"Yeah. Yeah it's a yes, Beth. It's a yes."

Bethany dropped her pen and the list, wrapped her arms around Savannah, and breathed into her neck. "Thank you. I promise I'll be a good wife. I promise."

She held her close, pressing her body against Savannah's while placing kisses all over her face and neck.

"I don't have a ring. I'm sorry. It was so spontaneous. But I will get you a ring, Savy. A big one. A shiny one with diamonds and everything."

"Shush," Savannah whispered. "I don't need a ring. Not now. Just kiss me."

10. Get a pink Christmas tree—check

11. Own a tiger—check

12. Design my own tattoo—check

# Chapter 12

"Could you move your leg a little? Yeah...like that..."

"Ouch. Ouch, my hair!"

"Sorry."

Bethany giggled.

"This is more difficult than it looks," Savannah growled as she tried to spread her legs further without falling out of the hammock. Bethany was lying on top of her, kissing her neck. Savannah's left hand was searching for anything she could hold on to while her right hand kept pleasuring Beth.

"If only it didn't swing so much," Bethany murmured. "Maybe if we move a little less."

"Your fingers are inside me, babe. How little do you expect me to move, huh?"

Bethany had to grin.

"Good point!" she admitted, kissing Savannah's nose before focusing on building up a steady rhythm again.

It was cold at the Indian Lake Beach but they both knew what to expect when they had decided to spend the night by the water in February.

The thick blanket wrapped around them probably made the whole hammock experience even more difficult, yet Bethany couldn't help but love it. She loved the wind in her hair, loved the sound of the small waves, loved being here with Savannah. Oh, and Tigger, of course, who was asleep in his box.

The hammock was tiny and didn't look very stable, but at least there were palm trees. And did it really matter? The night had already been lovely in its own way.

"Mm...don't stop, Beth!" Savannah moaned, digging her nails a little deeper into the soft skin of Bethany's back. The hammock started rocking harder with each and every one of Bethany's thrusts.

"Yeah...deeper..."

Bethany smirked, moving faster, deeper, harder as Savannah buried her hands in her hair and kissed her to muffle her own moans.

"So close," Savannah whispered, and Bethany watched the intense pleasure reflect on her features.

"Yes. Oh, fuck, Beth."

"Oh, fuck, Savy!" Bethany exclaimed. The hammock ripped away from the tree and they landed in the sand with a thud. Bethany lay on top of Savannah.

"Shit, Savy, are you okay?"

"We broke the hammock." There was a second's silence, then big grins brightened up their faces. They began to giggle uncontrollably.

Bethany wrapped them up in the blanket so they lay on the sand staring at the sky. "Turn on the radio," Savannah said. Tigger crawled out of his box, yawning. He looked around, obviously a little confused, before spotting his owners and lazily climbing on top of Savannah's belly. Savannah reached out her hand to pet the little guy behind his ears, causing the small cat to purr and snuggle even closer.

"He's so adorable."

"And he loves you," Bethany added while still searching for a channel on the old portable radio they had brought with them.

"Oh, it's the news. Turn up the volume."

They were both waiting for the football results. There wasn't much time left until the Super Bowl. When the anchor finally announced the results, the smiles were wiped off their faces.

"They lost," Savannah said, disappointed. "The Jets lost."

Bethany's gaze dropped.

"I guess we can forget that point on the list," Savannah said, but Bethany shook her head.

"No. They're going to win next year!"

There was no way that the Jets would screw up their bucket list. Nope. Bethany wouldn't accept this.

"Honey," Savannah whispered as she nuzzled her head against Bethany's shoulder, "I'm not going to be around for the next Super Bowl."

*Thanks a lot for the reminder.* Sometimes it made Bethany angry to hear Savannah say it. To hear her say the things she already knew but that she refused to accept. It made her want to push Savy away and hug her at the same time. It made her want to shake her. It made the little girl inside of her scream and shout, but she had to get used to it. She had to swallow down these feelings. Had to learn that there was a difference between hope and living in denial.

Sometimes the whole bucket list thing just felt like a big, fun adventure. Like two people in love doing silly things together to pass the time. Sometimes she truly forgot what it was really about. Would she be sitting at the beach all by herself a year from now? Would it be just her and the cat?

And a year... What was a year? A year was nothing. The year without Savannah had felt long and tiring, but the five months they had been together again had felt like only five weeks.

Bethany could feel her own hands starting to shake and quickly tried to distract her mind from it all. "I talked to Joan. She wants to come over next weekend to help us with the wedding invitations and initial preparations. We could watch the Super Bowl together anyway, if you want?"

"Yes. Sure. I'd like that," Savannah agreed. She squeezed Bethany's hand before bringing it up to her lips to kiss it. "And Beth?"

"Hm?"

"Baby, please don't stress yourself, okay? I know that there are certain things that we won't be able to do anymore."

There it was again. That terrible feeling she had pushed down more or less successfully until now. The hot, uncomfortable shock wave.

"And I don't mind. It's been great so far, completely awesome and magical. You know, not all wishes can come true. And they don't have to."

"But—"

"No, honey. I'm good as long as I have you...and Joan and Tigger!" she added with a wink. "And I don't need to see Machu Picchu, okay? Really."

Bethany swallowed hard, pulling the blanket up to her chin as she focused on staying calm.

"Okay," she whispered, feeling defeated. Powerless. It was not okay.

*It'll never be okay.*

Savannah was more than excited to see Joan again and to spend the day with her two best friends. Not even seeing Loredana was going to change her good mood, especially because these blood transfusions had become a lot more bearable since Bethany was back in her life.

Usually she read books or magazines during the procedure or turned up the volume on her iPod and tried to clear her head, but Bethany had insisted on coming with her this time. She wanted to distract her with funny stories and her positive attitude.

She was sitting in front of her, smiling and petting her leg, while Savannah could feel the fresh blood making her stronger and a little more energetic. Anemia was a typical side effect of cancer, especially after having been through chemo, but after the transfusions, she felt ready to tackle anything.

"What do you want to eat tonight?" Bethany asked, her eyes glowing. "I think we need some typical Super Bowl food—what do you say? Oh, we could build a whole stadium out of cheese and crackers and make an audience out of gummi bears!"

Savannah had to grin. "Whatever floats your boat, baby."

"And burgers," Bethany said. "Burgers and fries, of course. And lots of Coke. And Snickers. Peanut butter sandwiches and M&Ms!"

"That sounds very healthy," Savannah said. "What about breadsticks?"

"Absolutely!"

"So, when does Joan arrive? Did she tell you?" Savannah asked. She was looking at the blood bag connected to her arm and growing a little impatient.

"She already arrived. She'll be back home when we get out of here," Bethany said. "I told Mrs. McPherson to let her in, so she will have already showered and stuff. I guess J's happy that she can stay with us and doesn't have to stay at her mom's all the time."

"Yeah, I don't blame her."

Loredana arrived to check on the transfusion.

"Okay, looks like you're done here." She carefully removed the needle from Savannah's arm. "How are you feeling?"

"Good. Great actually, thanks."

"Any plans for tonight?" Loredana put a little cotton ball on the bleeding spot.

"We're going to watch the Super Bowl and—"

"Make some important preparations," Bethany finished off the sentence.

Savannah blushed. Then she noticed the curious look on Loredana's face.

"Yeah, about that." Savannah cleared her throat. "Not many people know about it yet, but Beth and I are going to get married. You'll get a proper invitation soon."

Loredana's eyes widened at her words, then a big smile brightened up her face.

"Oh my God!" she exclaimed. "That's the best news I have heard all day. I am so happy for you both."

She wrapped her arms around Savannah and held her close before turning to hug Bethany.

All of Savannah's worries that Loredana would give her a warning melted away. The way the doctor smiled and congratulated them was all the reassurance she needed that marrying Bethany was the right thing to do.

"Have you already set a date?" Loredana asked.

"March 28th," Savannah said. "We wanted a spring wedding, and it gives us enough time to plan everything. We're currently looking for the right location."

"I'm sure whatever place you choose is going to be perfect," Loredana assured her, and Savannah nodded happily.

On the way home, Savannah pictured all kinds of wedding scenarios in her head, imagined Bethany trying on a slew of amazing wedding dresses, and thought of all kinds of fancy hotel rooms where they would spend their honeymoon and never leave the bed. She hoped she would feel as strong then as she felt right now. She hoped her body would allow her to be a good wife for a good long time.

Mrs. McPherson was busy cleaning the path with her big red broom when they arrived at home. She stared at them with her typical grim expression.

"You have a visitor," she said before focusing on the pile of leaves at her feet again.

"Thanks," Bethany chirped happily and got the big box of groceries out of the trunk. "Are you going to watch the Super Bowl tonight, Mrs. M?"

The elderly woman only raised an eyebrow.

"Well, if you do, you should totally come over for a snack. We're going to build our own cracker stadium!"

"Can't wait." Mrs. McPherson stuffed the leaves into a big brown garbage bag.

"Geez, Beth, why are you always so nice to the old witch?" Savannah whispered as they walked up to their flat and she fumbled for her keys.

"I don't know. I think she's lonely, and I kinda like her. I think we should invite her to our wedding."

"And I think you're insane," Savannah replied dryly. "But I still love you."

Bethany smiled and kissed Savannah's cheek before pushing the door open.

"Holy fuck, J, what is this?" Savannah asked when she entered the apartment.

Joan had done a lot more than take a shower while they were gone. The whole apartment was decorated with green New York Jets flags and garlands. Everything was green, including the sofa, which was wrapped up in green sheets. It looked a little like a private St. Patrick's Day party.

"Welcome home, Savy," Joan said grinning. "Like it?"

"I do, but you're aware that we're about to watch Pittsburgh versus New Orleans tonight, right?" Savannah gave her friend a dubious look.

"We aren't," Bethany said. She shrugged before wrapping her arms around Joan to greet her. "It looks awesome, J. Score!"

"Okay, hold up. What have you two planned behind my back again?" Savannah wanted to know. "And why do you never include me in your crazy ideas beforehand?"

"Well, isn't it a lot more fun this way?" Joan took an old VHS tape out of her bag and threw it over to Savannah.

*Super Bowl 1969—New York Jets vs. Baltimore Colts* was written on it, and Savannah laughed.

"Ebay," Joan added, shrugging, before taking the groceries from Bethany and carrying them into the kitchen.

Bethany cleared her throat. "You wanted to see the Jets win the Super Bowl, but you didn't say which Super Bowl it had to be."

Savannah shook her head, laughing. "Bethany S. Peters, you truly are the master of all bucket lists. I'm fucking impressed!"

Bethany beamed before clapping her hands in excitement. "Wait 'til you see our outfits!"

"We thought it was time to relive the Trashy Triplets cheerleading spirit for one more evening," Joan said. She nodded in the direction of a big plastic bag on the dining room table. "Open it."

"Oh my God." Savannah gasped and took one of the uniforms out of the bag.

The original green Jets uniforms. And not only the usual short skirts. Somehow they had managed to get their hands on the dark green aviator overalls that the cheerleading squad always wore on special occasions.

"This is—"

"Genius? Silly?" Bethany asked slowly.

"Definitely genius. And it will look absolutely hot on you."

Joan chuckled. "Maybe I should sleep at my mom's place tonight so you two can appreciate those overalls a little more."

"No way." Savannah smiled. "You're staying. And thank you. Both of you."

"I've never actually seen Joe Namath play before tonight, but he was a fucking rock star!" Savannah said as she stroked her belly, which was full of Snickers, cheese, and breadsticks. The halftime show had just started, and the game had been very entertaining so far. Bethany was happy that Savannah seemed to be enjoying it.

"Time to pee." Savannah placed a quick kiss on Bethany's lips before disappearing into the bathroom.

Bethany leaned back on the sofa and sighed contently. "I'd say this has been a success so far."

"Absolutely. I don't even mind the horrible video quality. It's kind of classy." Joan smiled. "But Beth?"

"Hm?"

"I don't mean to be a mood killer, but..." She sighed. "She looks so thin."

"Savy?"

"Yeah. I mean, I haven't seen her in two months, so maybe it's more obvious to me than it is to you, but she looks very weak."

Bethany hugged her knees in front of her chest and pulled them closer to her body as she tried to smile back at Joan. Of course she had noticed it too. Of course she was trying not to think about it too much.

"She's not that weak, though," Bethany said. "Her doctor says she's still remarkably strong, and it's normal that she's losing weight. Her body needs a lot of energy, but she can't eat that much. She easily feels sick. She can't keep all the food down."

Joan nodded.

"But she's trying. She's doing the best she can to eat properly. I know that. Today was an exception," Bethany went on. "I know she's doing it for us, even if she's almost never hungry and quickly loses her appetite. And she barely ever complains, J. Sometimes I wish I could look into her head to know when she's in pain, you know? Because she doesn't talk about it. She doesn't want to make me worry."

They heard the bathroom door before Joan got a chance to reply, but she gave Bethany's arm a quick squeeze. There was a sad smile on her lips.

"What did I miss?" Savannah wanted to know. Joan lifted her phone, motioning her to sit down next to them.

"I was just about to post a pic of us on Facebook," Joan grinned and held up the phone camera in front of them. "Smile."

She uploaded the photo to her Facebook wall and added a comment: "Alternative Super Bowl rocks! Our party is better than yours!"

Only a few seconds later, the picture had twenty-seven likes and three comments, most of them coming from old high school friends they hadn't seen in years.

"It's weird, isn't it?" Savannah said slowly. "All these people. People we used to know so well. Now we know next to nothing about them, only what they give away on some stupid social network."

Joan nodded. "I know. The word 'friend' has totally lost its meaning on the Internet. But I know who my true friends are and who I really want to be part of my life. It's all that matters."

"Speaking of important people," Bethany said before grabbing a piece of paper she had left under the table, "we started the list for our wedding invitations. Do you want to see it?"

"Sure," Joan replied.

Bethany handed it to her. So far, only a few names were written on it: Anna, Bethany's colleague from work, Loredana, Bethany's parents, and, on Bethany's insistence, the lovely Mrs. McPherson.

"I want a small and very private wedding," Savannah whispered.

It was obvious from the list that there was no mention of Savannah's family.

"And there is no one else you want to have there with you, Savy?" Joan asked carefully. Savannah didn't look at her. She shook her head. Bethany and Joan gave each other a meaningful glance.

"Let's keep watching." Savy snuggled into Beth. The conversation was over.

After a glorious 16-7 victory, they headed over to the tattoo shop where they had made an appointment a couple of days before. They were still wearing their uniforms. It felt good to wear them together, like the old times. It made Savannah feel young again, as if she were back in high school.

High school. A time that seemed so far away. So far away from all these dark thoughts. A time when she still had huge plans for her future. Becoming successful. Living in New York. Having a huge family and growing old with Bethany.

It had always been clear to her that Bethany would be her partner forever. Her wife, even. But who would have thought that "always" could be so short? "Always" used to sound like an eternity.

Bethany would always be her girlfriend, but she wouldn't always be hers.

But that's what this tattoo was all about. That even if Savannah's "always" ended earlier than Bethany's, the girl she loved would still carry a piece of Savannah with her. Some small part of her would always be with her.

Bethany pressed her eyes shut when the needle came close to her pinky finger.

Joan laughed. "Believe me—getting the tattoo is a lot less painful than having it removed. I know what I'm talking about," she said, pointing at the spot on her lower back that used to be covered by Leonardo Di Caprio's face.

"Good thing I'll never have to remove this one," Bethany whispered.

Savannah bit the inside of her cheek when it was her turn to get inked, but it didn't hurt as much as she expected it to. Maybe she had gotten used to needles.

She looked over to Joan and thought she could see a tear in her friend's eye. Joan had always been a hopeless romantic on the inside, even if she didn't want to admit it. Savannah knew Joan was probably dwelling on the thought of her and Bethany getting a tattoo as a sign of their eternal love. Or maybe she was also taking this whole thing a lot harder than Savannah had expected.

Yeah. Suddenly, Savannah felt like Joan might be going to miss her a lot, almost as if this whole thing were breaking her heart.

For a second, their eyes met, but Joan quickly looked away and brushed the tear away with the sleeve of her uniform. Savannah was sure that Joan didn't want to ruin the mood by getting emotional, especially because it had been a cheerful night so far. Savannah wanted to get up and hug her. To tell her it was okay, that she didn't have to feel sorry for her. That she still had Bethany and that Bethany was the best friend anyone could wish for. That they could still be Trashy Twins together.

Savannah didn't get up. She looked at her two favourite blondes, realizing that the tattoo artist's job wasn't done yet.

"I'm sorry. I know that it's late and all, but do you think you could make me another tattoo, just a really small one on my neck?"

The tattooist, who was completely covered in ink herself, laughed. "I know that it can get addictive, but wow, it got you pretty fast!" she said with a wink. "What's it going to be?"

"I want a trinity symbol," Savannah said in a firm voice. And from the corner of her eye, she could see Joan smile.

When they came back home, Bethany decided it was time to talk about what everyone had avoided mentioning all night.

They lay on their bellies on Savannah's huge bed while flipping through wedding magazines and discussing the dresses that they liked the most.

Joan made a list of things that still needed to be arranged. It was obvious she was enjoying her unofficial job as wedding planner.

"Savy?" Bethany asked.

"Yeah?"

"Can we talk about the whale in the room? I know the word is 'elephant,' but it feels much bigger than that."

Savannah sighed. "I don't know what you're talking about." She focused her gaze on a catering brochure.

"Your parents, Savy. Your mom. Your grandma. I know that you want them to attend."

Joan put her magazine away. "Beth's right," she said. "It's about time, sweetie. It's going to be the most important day in your life. You're going to want your mom to be there. You're going to want your dad to walk you down the aisle, and you're going to want your grandma's blessing."

"I will never get her blessing," Savannah said, her voice cracking.

"You don't know that, babe," Bethany whispered. She rested her chin on Savannah's shoulder. "I'm sure they all miss you just as much as you miss them."

This was Savannah's weak spot. Savannah needed closure. Bethany felt it in her heart. She would never make Savy go through with it otherwise.

"And we're here for you, Savannah," Joan said with a smile on her lips. "We'll hold your hand. And we'll drive over there and kick their sorry asses in the very unlikely chance they push you away. Which is *not* going to happen."

Savannah's eyes were teary, and Bethany could see her inner struggle as if she could hear Savannah's heart beating in her own ears. But it was now or never.

"Give me the phone," Savannah said. She looked so vulnerable, it broke Bethany's heart.

"Hello?" Savannah's mother answered.

Bethany squeezed Savannah's hand until her knuckles were white. She could feel the tremor run through her.

"Mom?" Savy whispered, her voice sounding tiny.

Silence.

"Savannah? Is that you?"

Tears streamed down Savannah's face, and Bethany couldn't even begin to imagine what it must be like for her. What it must be like to tell your own mother that... She couldn't even finish the thought. All she knew was that she felt incredibly proud of Savannah in that moment. She admired her for being so strong. And she'd do anything for Savannah.

"Mom. I… I'm calling because…because there's something you need to know. Something I need to tell you—"

"Savannah, I've missed you. I've missed you so much."

Savannah closed her eyes shut and squeezed Bethany's hand.

"I've missed you too, Mom."

13. Have sex in a hammock between palm trees—check.

14. Watch the New York Jets win the Super Bowl—check.

# Chapter 13

SAVANNAH SAT ON A KITCHEN chair, her hands sweaty. The ticking of the blue clock on the kitchen wall was echoing loudly in her ears.

Tick. Tick. Tick.

Time seemed to pass so slowly.

Of course, she couldn't be sure that they'd really show up. Maybe they would change their minds. Maybe she was terrified over nothing.

Would she be disappointed if they stood her up? Right now, the thought seemed more like a relief.

How would she react if they did come? Would she shake their hands? Hug them? Maybe it was best to wait until they made the first move.

She had told Bethany that she needed to do this on her own. That she needed at least this one honest moment with her family. She was prepared for the questions they hadn't dared to ask yet. Right now, however, she wished she had let her stay. Bethany always calmed her down, made her feel safe. Just a small smile, a squeeze of her hand could make everything better.

The spoon in her hand was shaking as she stirred the cold coffee she didn't feel like drinking. When the doorbell finally did ring, she still managed to splash some coffee on the table. She could feel the heat in her face, and she tried to focus on her breathing as she pressed the buzzer. There was no turning back now.

Her mother came through the door first. Her hair was shorter. Grayer. Her eyes looked swollen.

The person with her wasn't her father. Savannah couldn't believe her eyes when she saw her *abuela* enter the room. The old lady looked at her with an expression Savannah wasn't able to read, even if she had wanted to.

"Good evening, Savannah," her abuela said.

So here they were, the two people who had meant the most to her during her childhood. The two people who had disappointed her more than anybody else. They were supposed to love her no matter what, and they had also decided that they didn't want her anymore—her mother because of her life choices, her grandmother because of who she loved. Even after all these years, the pain still felt as real as it had always felt. The rejection. The anger. It all bubbled to the surface.

But now there was something else too. Now there was this new fear. The fear of dying. And Savannah wasn't quite sure what role her family would play in all this. What role she would *let* them play.

How much longer were they going to stand there and look at her? Was this the time to offer them a drink? Maybe this had been a bad idea. Joan and Bethany shouldn't have pushed her, for fuck's sake. This was going to make her feel even more miserable than she already felt. She could have waited the last few months and died without them. After death, there was no regret, right? At least not for her.

Then, suddenly, there were arms around her, an embrace that was so unexpected, it made her whole body tense within less than a second.

Her abuela still used the same perfume. Savannah had never particularly liked it. It smelled like cedarwood. Yet it smelled like home. Like childhood. And her arms felt so much skinnier. She looked so old. So weak.

"*Querida, querida,*" Savannah heard her grandmother mumble as she kissed her on the forehead. Once. Twice.

"Your father will come a little later," her mother, Gloria, explained. "He's still in a meeting. He says he's really sorry and that he will hurry."

They all knew that there was no meeting. Fernando Cortez wasn't able to deal with these kinds of emotions. And it was okay. To some degree, Savannah was thankful.

She had no idea how long they had been sitting there before Savannah finally had the nerve to speak. "I'm getting married to a girl." These hadn't exactly been the first words she had planned to say, but it was what had to come out.

"I'm getting married to a girl," she repeated, "and I can't help but feel that you wouldn't be here now if you didn't think it might be the last chance to see me. Alive, I mean."

She could feel her abuela freeze. Her hand had been stroking her seconds ago and was now resting still on her dark hair.

"That's not true, Savannah," her mother said slowly, and her eyes were getting teary. "It's not true, and I hope you know that."

"I don't, actually."

"Savannah," her abuela said in a strict voice that allowed no backtalk. "Savannah, look at me."

She didn't want to look at her. Didn't want to look into the eyes of the woman who had made her doubt herself so badly, the person whose opinion had always mattered so much to her but who had decided to stop loving her because she was a lesbian. Who had let her down when she had needed her most.

"It's been six years, Savannah. Six years since I have seen you. Six long years, and that's been more than enough time for me to think about you and our family."

Yeah, six fucking years that would have felt like hell if she hadn't had Bethany by her side. Six years and her abuela hadn't once tried to contact her to apologize.

"You have to believe me, Savannah. It isn't just now that I've realized I made a mistake. There have been many days, many situations, in which I have wanted to call you, write you, and I didn't do it because…because I was ashamed. Yes. There, I said it. I was ashamed of the way I have treated you, and I didn't know what to do. I figured it would be hard for you to forgive me, so I thought I would have to let you live your life with…with your *partner* and let you be happy."

Savannah could hear her voice crack, something she wasn't used to when it came to her grandmother, the woman who had an opinion on everything and who would never let any weakness show. In so many ways, they were very alike. Always had been.

"It was my own punishment, Savannah. To live with the thought that I had let you down in the worst way possible. Telling you all of those things when I knew how upset you must have been. I am not proud of that."

Tears were rolling down Savannah's cheeks as she tried to focus on the white kitchen floor. She was doing her best to push away the memories that came crawling back, memories of the time when she had tried to be brave and open up to her family about her most personal emotions, the memory of the hurt she had felt when her own grandmother had kicked her out. The memory of the pure hatred in the woman's eyes.

There had been too many days and nights she had spent denying who she really was, telling herself it was sick to feel the way she did. She had been her own worst enemy, had needed nothing more than to find comfort with her loved ones. Instead, they had rejected her and made her world fall into pieces. All she had ever wanted was an apology.

"I'm sorry, Savannah. And I hope you will be able to forgive me."

Savannah let the words sink in, not knowing what to reply. She wasn't ready for a "yes," yet there was a small smile tugging on her lips.

"Savannah," Gloria now started, her voice shy. "I…um…we, your grandmother and I, would love to help you pick a wedding dress." Suddenly, Gloria started sobbing, unable to hold back the emotions that must have kept her awake since the night of their phone call. "I've always dreamt of the moment when my baby girl would get married. How beautiful she'd look in a white dress. How proud I'd feel."

It broke Savannah's heart to see her mother cry like that. Maybe it was for the best that she would never have any children of her own. She only had to look into Gloria's eyes to know that losing your son or daughter to cancer was an experience she'd never want to go through.

"So, Savannah," her abuela said as she softly stroked Savannah's arm. "What do you say? Going to let your old ladies help you pick an outfit for the most important day of your life?"

Savannah swallowed and slowly lifted her head before clearing her throat to answer.

"You better not make me regret this."

Bethany wasn't allowed to see Savannah in her dress before the wedding, yet she did not want to waste a single day without her anymore. They had agreed that she could come with them as long as she closed her eyes or turned around whenever Gloria or Savannah's grandmother opened the curtain of the fitting room.

Of course the "oohs" and "ahs" of the two women kept making her want to peek, yet Bethany was sure that this meant bad luck, so she stayed strong and occupied herself with some iPhone game in which you had to help a crocodile get enough water for his daily bubble bath. A maddening game.

"Damn it, Swampy. Why do you have to live down there in the sewers anyway?" she mumbled, annoyed. "It's dark there, and it stinks!"

Gloria sat down next to Bethany as Savannah discussed with her abuela which dress made her boobs look bigger.

"You okay?" Gloria asked.

"No. I'm stuck in level twenty-seven. You wanna try?"

Gloria smiled. "I doubt that I'm any good at this. Though that's not exactly what I meant."

Bethany put the phone away into her pocket. "I'm okay," she replied, though she wasn't sure who she wanted to convince, Gloria or herself. "I'm glad you're here," Bethany continued. "Savannah wanted you here. Even if she doesn't admit it. It means a lot to her. And to me."

Gloria leaned back in her chair. Her gaze wandered to the dressing room. "I feel thankful," she said.

Thankful? For what, exactly? Bethany had always been a very positive person, but even she had started to forget what to be thankful for these days. She was lucky to still have Savannah, lucky she was getting married to her. But thankful? She would be thankful for a sudden cure.

"I feel thankful because…" Gloria swallowed, "because I know she has you in her life, Bethany. She's had you when we haven't been around. And you've been doing all these incredible things with her. I'm beyond thankful that she got to experience true friendship. That she got to experience true love."

Bethany nodded, a tiny smile on her lips.

"I want you to know something. And I'm not sure when else I'd get the chance to tell you, so I'd rather tell you now." Gloria sighed. "You're my daughter too, Bethany."

Bethany felt Gloria's hand on hers. Warm but a little shaky.

"Whenever it…whenever it will…I…" Gloria struggled to get the words out. "You're not alone. You'll always be a part of this family, and you'll always be welcome in our home. Don't forget that, okay?"

"I won't," Bethany replied. She wished she could help Swampy again, because she wasn't supposed to get sad now. Not today. She was shopping for a wedding dress, or at least she was around people who were shopping for one, and there was no room for sadness that might bubble to the surface at any second.

Gloria's hand was still on hers when Savannah's voice echoed out of the dressing room. "Mom! Get in here! I think we found it."

The following weeks had been quite eventful.

Joan, the unofficial, self-announced wedding planner, was having serious problems with Gloria's very strong opinion on everything. Gloria wanted everything to be pink, while Joan preferred yellow. Joan voted for a band, and Gloria insisted on a DJ.

Bethany and Savannah had often been worried that Joan and Gloria would end up in an embarrassing catfight.

Whenever they asked Bethany and Savannah to make the final decision, both of them agreed that they trusted their wedding planners and that they were both doing a great job.

Of course, Savannah realized that, in front of her, everyone was trying to act as if everything were okay and under perfect control. No one wanted to upset her.

A few months ago, Savannah *would* have been upset. She would have wanted to plan these things on her own, if only to show them that she needed no help. But something inside of her had changed.

It would have been enough to have a small wedding, to sit at Toni's Pizza Place with their closest friends. It didn't matter. Savannah was thankful for every minute she could spend with Bethany, was thankful that she knew she could trust her mom and her friends to arrange the things they felt were important for her wedding.

For her, it wasn't about the greatest cake or the best music anymore. It was about Bethany, soon to be her wife. And her family. And Joan. It wasn't the party that mattered as much as the people celebrating it with her.

The only thing truly upsetting Savannah was the fact that her dress didn't fit anymore. In only a few weeks, she had lost far too much weight. It felt as if the dress were swallowing her when she put it on.

Her abuela was standing next to her, their eyes meeting in the mirror. Tears were starting to blur Savannah's vision.

"C'mere," her abuela whispered. "Let me fix this."

Grabbing needle and thread, she looked at Savannah again, an encouraging smile on her lips. "No time for tears. My granddaughter is getting married. I want to see her smile."

For a while, she hadn't been sure that she'd be able to do it. There had been days when she had been feeling too weak. Days when she had been sure that they had to cancel on all their guests. Days when she preferred rolling around in the wheelchair they had got her— just in case. For there were many days that weighed heavy on her shoulders.

But now, when Savannah carefully stepped into the church and saw Bethany standing next to the altar, a new wave of power washed through her, right down to her bones. For a moment the pain seemed to be gone.

Her father's strong hands held her tightly on her right. Joan was walking by her left side, their fingers entwined. Nothing could happen to her. She was safe with them. Savannah looked around the church and realized that a lot of people had come. Old friends and work colleagues smiled encouragingly at her. The church was almost full. And then her eyes met Bethany's. Blue comfort. Filled with so much love.

Her father placed a kiss on her forehead before sitting down in the front row next to Gloria and her grandmother. Bethany's mother was smiling at her and carefully dried a tear with her pink hanky.

Bethany took her hand, and Savannah could feel her pulse speed up. Bethany leaned in and whispered into Savannah's ear. "You look so beautiful. I can't wait to say *I do*."

The reverend asked, "Miss Peters, Miss Cortez, are you ready?"

Savannah smiled and took Bethany's hands. "I'm ready."

"Courage is not the absence of fear. It means allowing yourself to be scared and allowing yourself to let love guide you, no matter what," the reverend began.

"There you go." Loredana was done with the injection. "It'll help you enjoy the next few hours a little more."

"Thank you," Savannah replied, relieved to feel the painkiller immediately taking effect.

Loredana had taken her into a side room to administer the injection. Savannah didn't want her guests to worry about her. The bass of the music was surrounding her, and she took a deep breath before leaving the room. The party had been fun, but Savannah was also looking forward to being in bed with Bethany.

"There she is," she heard Joan call. Her friend seemed to be enjoying herself a lot.

Joan got up, stumbled over to the DJ, and whispered something into his ear. He nodded and handed her his microphone. She cleared her throat and tapped her index finger on the mic several times. "Is this on? Hello?"

A loud beep was echoing through the speakers, which resulted in a few guests groaning and putting their hands over their ears. "I think it is. Fantastic." Joan slurred.

"Well," she started, a little louder this time. She smiled as she tapped her glass with a fork so hard that Savannah was afraid she'd break it. At least there was a doctor in the house, just in case Joan cut herself. "As the maid of honor, I think it's time for me to make a speech."

"What we have all been waiting for." Gloria rolled her eyes.

"I'm sorry, what was that?" Joan spoke into her microphone and took a step closer toward the bride's mother. "You were saying something, Gloria?"

Gloria shook her head and reached for her champagne. "Nothing."

"Nothing?" Joan repeated, faking a shocked expression. "That would be a first time!" she said before losing control and laughing out loud. Then she hiccupped.

"Oh I'm sorry, it's just—it's just that you should know that Savannah's mother has an opinion on everything. I won't blame her. It's her daughter's wedding, after all. Yeah."

Joan stumbled, barely managed to hold her balance, and started to laugh again.

"You sure you're okay?" the DJ said as he came over.

"I am fine. F-I-N-E!" Joan pushed him away. "I am fine because my best friends are married now, and I wanna say a few words, so puh-leaaase let me."

Savannah looked over at Bethany, who seemed very amused by all this. She was giggling and staring at their friend excitedly. Savannah had a weird feeling in her belly. She had known Joan long enough to know that this could easily turn into a disaster.

"Bethany and Savannah!" Joan continued. "Savannah and Bethany. Savethany. Or Bethannah? Whatever you guys prefer." She cleared her throat, and Savannah was worried Joan was going to puke in front of all of their guests.

"Who would have thought that they'd get married? I mean, ten years ago they were the most popular girls at school, dating all the guys, sometimes at the same time—but hey, I always knew what was going on during those sleepovers. Wink, wink."

Some people laughed, but most were looking awkwardly at their tables or drinks.

"And look at them. Seriously. They are both gorgeous. Gorgeous girls—nah, women. Let's face it. We're not getting younger, are we?" Joan seemed to be staring aimlessly, lost in thought, though she was smiling. "We're not getting younger, but that's the point of getting married, right? We decide that we have found the right person to grow old with. We stop caring about age. Because…because no matter how old we are, we love this one person. Even if he or she has wrinkles or is getting bald. We know we want to wake up next to this person for the rest of our lives."

Her tone was becoming more serious, and Savannah glanced over to Bethany again. The smile had been washed off her face, replaced by, well, what was it? She didn't look sad. She was just staring at Joan, hanging onto every word.

"You know what the best-case scenario is?" Joan asked the audience, though she didn't seem to want an answer. "The best-case scenario is that your spouse is also your best friend." Suddenly there were tears in her eyes.

"And this is what these two have—a friendship which has always been so close, untouchable, even. Of course, I've always been their friend as well, but what those two had? It was special. Still is." She paused. "It's something everyone in this room can be jealous of."

Savannah looked around the room to see how Joan's little performance was going down. Some people were nodding, most of them looked sad and serious.

"It's this deep friendship that brought them back together. And, fuck, it will always unite them, okay? Have you seen their tattoos?"

Savannah was close to walking over to Joan and telling her that it was okay and that she could stop talking now. But somehow she couldn't move. Somehow Joan seemed to have everyone under a spell.

"Let me tell you something. If I'm ever lucky enough to find a love like what Bethany and Savannah have, I will die happy. Because I think this is what we're here for on this miserable little place called Earth."

Joan was slurring again, the occasional sobs making it even harder to understand her. "We're here for love. To experience it with our whole heart and soul." She slumped into an ungainly heap on the floor, sitting and staring out into the crowd until she locked her gaze with Savannah's.

"Savannah," she reached her hand out to Bethany, "Beth," she said.

Savannah stepped closer to Bethany and held her hand.

"I love you, girls. So much. Okay?" Joan brushed a tear away with her sleeve. "And it's an honor to be your maid of honor." She paused. "Wow. Suddenly the title makes sense."

Savannah smiled.

"I haven't said it before, but I will say it now, because I'm drunk as fuck, okay?"

*Uh-oh.* Savannah stiffened, her grip on Bethany tightening.

"I don't know what I'll do once… I really don't know. I just…"

Savannah felt Bethany squeeze her hand back.

"It just hurts to think about… It hurts. I just want you to… I want to come over to your house when we're all, like, ninety-five or something. I want to see your children and spoil them with presents and be their favorite aunt. I want all that for you two. The whole thing. The real deal. I'm… Oh God, I'm sorry."

Savannah had never seen Joan like this before. She knew that whatever else Joan wanted to say, whatever else she felt, it was too strong for words. Especially now.

"Excuse me, please." The microphone dropped to the floor, and Joan ran out of the room. She was pushing some guests out of her way as she tried to get through to the door without meeting Savannah's gaze.

Two hours later, most of the guests had left. Bethany had tried calling Joan, but she hadn't picked up her phone. At some point, Joan had sent a text.

*I'm so sorry. I hope you know that. It was a beautiful wedding and I love you girls. I'll call you in the morning. Have a great night. xx*

They weren't mad at her. How could they be? The day had been beautiful, it really had, and Joan had done her best to make all of this happen. The weather had been perfect, the decorations had been stunning, the food delicious. They had danced, Bethany's head resting on Savannah's shoulder. They had laughed. They had seen all of their friends, and Bethany knew how much Savannah had enjoyed their hugs, their friendly faces. She had wanted to see them one more time, had wanted to celebrate this with them.

Now Bethany could see how tired Savannah was. She was very pale, but she was also happy.

In the moonlight flooding their bedroom, she stepped behind Savannah to open the zipper of her wedding dress, let it fall down to the floor, and helped Savannah step out of it. She drifted kisses along her shoulder and felt the flesh tremble under her lips.

Savannah was her wife now. That was all that mattered.

It felt as if time had stopped. And there was nothing she wanted to do but lie down beside her and listen to the sound of Savannah breathing, to the sound of her heartbeat, so in time with her own. Bethany wanted to appreciate every second of it. She wanted to cling to this sliver of time.

Savannah's skin was so soft. So unbelievably soft. And she was warm. And she smelled fantastic. Bethany felt so much comfort lying in her arms.

There was no way that it could ever feel different. Because this was the woman she loved with all her heart, with everything she had, and she needed her by her side. How would she live without her?

Bethany let her head rest on Savannah's breast while Savannah stroked her hair. She felt her head move up and down…up and down with each inhalation. She felt so incredibly close to her.

Savannah wrapped her arms around Bethany and held her tight. There was no need to speak. Bethany already knew what Savannah was feeling, what she wanted to say—"I'm still here for you."

*Please don't go. Pretty fucking please, don't leave me alone, please.* The panic clawed at her. Then she felt the soft kiss on her forehead and closed her eyes. The panic receded.

*You weren't supposed to feel like this on your wedding night, were you?*

But then again, what was a wedding about in the first place? For Bethany it was simple—two people wanting to spend the rest of their lives together. Bethany knew that Savannah was the one for her. That she'd always be her forever person.

Memories flashed by. Childhood days. High school days. First Kiss. First Fight. First Sex. Savannah laughing. Savannah healthy.

Darkness was surrounding them. She felt more than shadows creeping in. "Thank you for being my wife," Bethany whispered into the silence.

Savannah softly stroked Bethany's neck, and it was the most comforting feeling in the world. "I love you more than anything, and this has been the best day of my life," Savannah replied.

Slowly, Savannah closed her eyes, though Bethany knew she felt just as wide awake as she did herself.

That was all they said that night.

There wasn't really much more to say.

15. Talk to my grandmother again—check.

16. Be your wife—check.

# Chapter 14

"LOOK AT THE CAMERA, SAVY! Oh yes, that's perfect! Oh my God, you'll be so impressed when I show you these at home!" Bethany giggled excitedly, her thumb swiping from one picture to the next as she admired the perfect snapshots she had taken of her wife in the water next to a dolphin named Lola.

The lady from Dolphin Therapy assured them Lola would take really good care of her wife. Savannah looked so happy in the pictures.

"Beth, you should come back inside and put that camera away," Savannah told her. Bethany could see the joy in her eyes. That spark that hadn't left her since the day they had said "I do" to each other.

They had been married for more than two months now, and even though Savy had been too weak to travel anywhere for their honeymoon, they had tried to enjoy each day to the fullest. They had decorated Savannah's wheelchair together, and Bethany had rolled her around in the park, by the lake, or wherever she wanted to go. Loredana had checked in on them almost every night, to make sure she could help Savannah with the pain. And she had explained to Bethany everything she needed to know about the infusion so she could help too.

Bethany was brought back to reality when Lola splashed some water in her direction, followed by the ridiculously cute sound that Bethany thought must have been actual dolphin giggles. "Okay, okay, I'm coming," she told the animal and put her camera back into her backpack before carefully climbing back into the pool.

"There you are," Savannah whispered and pulled her closer. "Kiss me."

Bethany smiled into the kiss, enjoying Savannah's wet skin on her own. She was delighted to have found the dolphin therapy online, and she could tell that it was really working. It allowed Savannah to get rid of her oxygen tubes for an hour or two, and they were surrounded by professionals, which made Bethany feel much safer about the whole thing.

One of the employees helped Savannah out of the water and handed her a towel, which she wrapped around her shivering shoulders. There were goose bumps on her thin legs, and it sounded as if her teeth were chattering, but Savannah didn't seem to mind.

"I can't wait for tonight," she said, trying to suppress coughing. "It's going to be magical, Beth-Beth."

Bethany smiled.

They were going to see the July 4th fireworks on a helicopter tonight. A gift from the supervisor of Dolphin Therapy. He had also arranged for them to spend the night at the aquarium, as well as a private koala feeding for Savannah several days ago. Bethany had kept the picture of Savannah and the fluffy little bear in her wallet ever since.

"I can't wait either," she said and carefully rubbed Savannah's shoulders dry.

It had been a warm and sunny day, and they could go out without a jacket and enjoy the soft summer breeze on their skin.

The copilot helped them adjust their helmets, and Savannah grinned at Bethany with the bright green helmet on her head.

"We have to take a picture now," she said as she held her phone in front of their faces. "Smile!"

They sent the selfie to Joan, with a short message.

> *About to have a magnificent night. Helicopter. Fireworks.*
> *We miss you! Love is in the air!*

The answer came back seconds later.

> *I love you girls. Enjoy! Xoxo*

Bethany grabbed Savannah's hand and squeezed it tightly as they left the ground. The world underneath them was getting smaller, and the feeling was truly magical.

"You okay?" Bethany yelled into her mic.

Savannah nodded excitedly. "Look around you, Beth. This is fucking fantastic." And it was.

They were positioned at a safe distance when their view suddenly filled with bursts of color. The music they had picked beforehand was buzzing in their ears through their headphones.

A wave of emotion rushed through Savannah as she looked at the colorful sparks reflecting in Bethany's beautiful eyes. She had forgotten her pain, had forgotten the knot that usually felt so tight in her chest. Time had stopped. This was easily becoming the best night of her life.

"I love you, Bethany Peters."

Bethany smiled. "I love you too, Savannah Cortez."

Savannah watched the rockets rising up into the air before bursting in the night's sky and leaving a trail of stardust and awe. Then the magic burned up and simply disappeared. *Some things shine brightest before leaving the world for good.*

Bethany stroked the back of Savannah's hand with her thumb throughout the entire performance and hopped excitedly in her seat whenever an especially beautiful scenario painted the sky right before their eyes. Savannah loved the golden glitter most, the one that Bethany referred to as "unicorn poop."

They landed safely, and Bethany and the pilot helped Savannah get out of the helicopter. Her wheelchair was already waiting for her, and Savannah couldn't deny that she would need a blast of fresh oxygen soon.

"There's one thing we need to do first, though," Bethany said with a smile, and Savannah teared up at the sight of the two floating lanterns that one of the staff members had already prepared for them while they'd been up in the air.

"Perfect, Beth. A perfect way to end this night."

Bethany nodded. "I felt it had to be tonight." She pointed at the little piece of paper that was attached to the lanterns. "Write your wish."

She handed Savannah a pen. What was the chance that these wishes really came true? She knew it probably didn't make sense to wish for a happy end, but maybe, if she played her cards right, a little faith might make anything possible.

She looked over at Bethany who was eagerly scribbling onto her paper, her tongue sticking out in concentration. If she was honest with herself, all she had ever wished for was for Bethany to be happy.

But tonight she had to think of herself for once. Tonight she wanted to make a wish that she had never dared to make before. She swallowed hard when the tip of the pen touched the paper.

There were tears in her eyes when she lit the small candle inside the balloon.

"On the count of three!" Bethany said. And three seconds later, their lanterns started floating and dancing together in the sky before slowly disappearing in the distance.

"What did you wish for? Wait, don't tell me, or it won't become true," Bethany said before grabbing Savannah's hand.

Savannah had to look the other way. She closed her eyes and bit her bottom lip in order to get rid of the lump in her throat.

When she looked up again, the sky was finally dark.

Back home, Savannah rested on the couch and was browsing through the bucket book, lost in thought. She let her index finger run along the picture of Bethany in her wedding dress before turning the page and putting some glue on the photo of herself and Lola in the dolphin tank. It had been a fantastic Fourth of July. She remembered the fireworks and helicopter ride with a huge, satisfied smile.

Tigger was climbing up her arm and started meowing into her ear while leaving little scratch marks on her skin.

"Ouch." She carefully placed him on her lap. "You're getting bigger, little tiger. Be careful with those dangerous claws!"

The cat looked at her as if he understood before snuggling closer to her belly. He started purring softly as she stroked his back.

"On the other hand," she deliberated out loud, tickling Tigger's ears, "you better keep them claws sharp. Once I'm gone, it'll be your job to take care of Bethany, you hear me? It'll be much easier to leave her behind knowing that a fully grown tiger is protecting her in her sleep." When he started licking her hand, Savannah rolled her eyes. "See, that's the kind of mean behavior I was talking about."

She had just written *swimming with a dolphin* next to one of the photos when she felt her phone vibrate. She looked at the screen. One message from Loredana read: *have you talked to her yet? What does she say?*

Savannah closed her eyes. She wasn't in the mood for this now. She didn't think she'd ever be in the mood to have that talk.

*Not now. Talk to you tomorrow–S*, she texted back before stuffing the phone underneath the blanket that was lying next to her.

The next vibration was barely audible and much easier to ignore. She took a deep breath in order to avoid another coughing fit. She failed.

Savannah reached for a tissue. Her lungs felt as if they were about to collapse. She held the white handkerchief in front of her face and cringed when she saw the blood.

"You okay, baby?" she heard Bethany yell from the bathroom. The shower had stopped, and there was some steam coming out from under the door.

"I'm fine," she called out, still choking a little. "All good."

When Bethany came into the room, wrapped in her yellow bathrobe, Savannah quickly shoved the bloody tissue under the sofa. She'd throw that away later.

"Want me to get you your green tea?" Bethany asked.

"Why don't you just sit with me for a bit?" Savannah replied and patted the spot next to her on the couch. "Oh, I'm sorry, with *us*," she corrected when she saw Tigger's indignant glare.

Bethany giggled and sat down. She didn't need to be told twice.

"You looking at our book again?" she asked before letting her head rest on Savannah's shoulder.

"Yeah."

"I think it's pretty much the coolest thing we ever did together," Bethany said proudly. "What's been your favourite bucket point so far?"

Savannah thought about the question for a moment before shaking her head. "It's impossible to choose." She went through the book from the beginning and had to smile when she saw the very first picture. "This is already one of my favourites."

"The motorcycle?" Bethany asked incredulously. "It was just a toy. I mean, it was supposed to be a little thing to get us started."

"I know. That's what I love about it." She took Bethany's hand into her own and softly kissed her fingertips. "I will never forget what I felt in that moment. You were wearing this leather jacket, and you looked so incredibly sexy." She had to laugh. "I hadn't been around you in so long, and I had missed you so fucking much. And there you were, looking hot as hell, being so unbelievably cute about the whole situation, even though I had been a total bitch."

She became serious. "After all the crying, all the worrying, all this shitty loneliness, you managed to give me butterflies again. Just like that. That's who you are, and it's exactly why I love you so much."

"I had butterflies too. Even though I was terrified. It's a strange combination," Bethany replied.

Savannah turned the page. "Oh my God," she laughed. "Remember the bus?"

"One of my favorite adventures with you."

"For sure," Savannah agreed. "I can't believe almost a year has passed since then."

"We finally kissed."

"Uh-huh."

They both smiled at the memory, and Savannah was convinced that this had been the best kiss of her life. The flashback hit her hard. She wished she could turn back time, relive it all again.

It had rained, and she'd run Bethany's wet hair through her fingertips. The excitement. The relief. The thought that anything was possible opened up to her that day. For a moment she'd believed they would conquer it all. That they could kick the cancer's ass as long as they had each other.

She was so—so—fucking thankful for having met Bethany again in that hair salon. So thankful for the past year. For their journey and the joy it had brought her. The light at the end of her godforsaken tunnel.

Bethany leaned closer to kiss Savannah's ear. It sent a shiver down her spine.

On the next page was a picture of Joan, and it warmed Savannah's heart a little more.

"What a party," Bethany murmured as she looked at the photo. "Vegas rocks!"

"I can still see you on that dance floor. Feel you, even," Savannah added. She wished she could dance with her wife once more. They had always loved to dance whenever and wherever possible. No one had the moves like Bethany.

"I'm still dancing with you in my dreams." Bethany smiled, though Savannah could see her chin shivering slightly.

"I was so happy that you brought Joan back into my life that day. I hadn't realized how much I missed her."

"And I'm glad we got those tattoos together," Bethany said. "Something that'll always unite us."

They locked their pinkies, the words written on them fading into one message that had become some sort of mantra to them. *Love, forever unbroken.*

A sound from underneath the blanket interrupted them.

"Savannah, your phone keeps vibrating. Maybe you should pick it up," Bethany said, a slightly worried look on her face.

"It's only Lory, Beth."

"What does she want? You said she didn't have time to come over tonight. I thought she was celebrating with her family?"

Savannah sighed. "Bethany, I…I didn't want to do this tonight. But we agreed to always be honest, so…" She cleared her throat and had to cough again.

Bethany frowned. "What now, Savy? It can't be that bad, can it? Not considering what we're already dealing with every day."

Savannah bit her bottom lip. "She wants to talk about several…um… *options* with us."

"Options?" Bethany asked, a confused look on her face. "I'm not sure I know what you mean."

"Babe." Savannah sighed and avoided Bethany's eyes. "I meant stuff like, you know, stationary hospices, palliative stations, that sort of thing. A nice place with experienced staff who can help when it gets down to… They can help us make it easier." Savannah could see Bethany swallow. Could see the tears in her eyes.

"Don't say it. Say no more," Bethany whispered. "Not tonight."

Savannah smiled and carefully removed the oxygen tubes from her nose before dragging her in for a hug.

"You're right." She kissed the damp blonde hair that she loved so much. "Not tonight. We can deal with it some other day."

She felt Bethany nod against her chest and knew that she wasn't able to speak now. And that was okay. For the moment she just wanted to keep Bethany warm and safe beside her, because that was where she belonged.

"Beth?"

"Hm?"

"I just wanted you to know that I'm really happy. This was a beautiful day. One of the best days of my life. And that's because of you."

Bethany looked at Savannah and brushed a tear off her cheek.

She smiled back. "Yes. It was beautiful."

Savannah carefully tried to drag Bethany up so they were on eye level again. She leaned closer to touch her chin with her thumb before kissing her. Bethany's lips parted as she responded to the kiss, and their tongues met almost shyly. Every kiss with Bethany felt like a first kiss. A little hurricane in her belly. The excited tickle over her skin. Her heart thumping in her throat instead of her chest. And the thought of doing this until time ended was magical.

Savannah let her forehead rest against Bethany's and kept stroking her hair. She wanted to tell her, without words, that everything would be okay.

"I'm getting really tired, Savy. And you must be exhausted."

"I'll stay awake a little longer. Until you fall asleep, okay? Let's go to bed."

They moved to the bedroom where Bethany took off her bathrobe and climbed under the sheets. Savannah quickly followed her. When Bethany turned around to find her typical sleeping position, Savannah came closer to spoon her tightly.

"Hold my hand?" Bethany asked.

Savannah smiled and had their fingers entwined in front of Bethany's belly in an instant. The most comforting feeling in the world.

"Sleep now, baby. I'll watch over you," Savannah whispered.

She kissed her hair until Bethany finally closed her eyes and let out a deep and content sigh.

"You know I always will." Savannah waited until she heard Beth's soft little snore. She watched her sleep for what felt like an eternity. Then she grabbed her phone and left the room.

When Bethany opened her eyes again, it was already bright outside. She felt Savannah lying next to her and immediately turned around to wake her. It was a Sunday, and she would prepare breakfast for them. Maybe they could stop by the lake again later. Maybe they could call Joan.

Savannah looked content, but something was different. Usually Savannah would hide her face as soon as the room turned bright. Sometimes she even put on her sleeping mask so no annoying ray of sunlight could interrupt her much valued sleep.

"Savy?" Bethany whispered. "Savy, please wake up."

Bethany's heart stopped.

No.

"Savannah!" she screamed, grabbing her hand. But it was cold. It was too fucking cold. "No. No, no, no, no, no…please, no." The last *no* was no more than a tortured whisper.

What now? What to do? Who to call? Fuck. Fuck, fuck, fuck, goddammit, fuck!

Bethany frantically searched for her phone. Her hands were shaking, and her legs turned to pudding. *Gotta call Lory. Gotta call 911. Gotta call someone. Anyone. Please.*

When she finally found her phone, she nervously pressed the home button and saw a message on her screen. A message from Savannah.

She opened it as fast as she could. Her whole body was shaking, and the tears were making it hard to read.

> *Baby, please don't cry. Don't call anyone. Not yet. We both knew that it had to happen. And I wanted it this way. I wanted to be with you. Please watch the video—I love you more than anything.*

It was so surreal. Sobs were shaking through her like hiccups. Yet, Bethany somehow managed to open the video that was attached to the message. Savannah smiled at her from the screen, and it felt like a knife in her chest. She had to force herself to listen as Savannah spoke to the camera.

"Hey." Savannah smiled, so unsure and insecure. "You are watching this message. That means it all worked out and…and we're finally free. I—I don't even know how to begin to tell you how unbelievably sorry I am. So sorry for what you have to face now. I can't even begin to imagine what it must feel like, being in your position." She looked away for a moment, gathering her thoughts.

"Bethany." Her gaze was back and level. "You always told me that you thought I was brave—but what does being brave even mean? It's not the absence of fear, it's facing your fears, right? It means being scared but still trying to go on and live your life to the fullest. And yeah, that's what we did. It's what we did together, Beth. You were the one who helped me face those fears. You're the reason why I didn't give up, why the worst year of my life also became the best year of my life. And you know what? I'm finally not scared anymore."

Her eyes shone with unshed tears. "I was scared of so many things. I was scared of the pain. Scared of being alone. Of dying alone. And what I was scared of the most was what it would all do to you. I was scared of leaving you behind, causing you pain, disappointing you." Here a single tear escaped and slid slowly down her cheek.

"I needed you in my life, babe. I needed you, and you were there for me, every step of the way. And now I'm gone and can't be there for you anymore the way that I want to be. But I'm also not scared that you won't make it, because I know you will. You're the strongest person I know. The bravest and most beautiful and most kind-hearted person I've ever met. And you will get through this, honey. Yes, you will. And I'll always be with you. I promise you." More tears joined the first. "I'll be more than just a little tattoo on your pinky or a ring on your finger. I'll be more than just a picture on your wall. I'll be everywhere around you. And there might be a point in time when you don't need me anymore. A point in time when you let somebody else love you—that lucky bitch!" Her attempt at a laugh was weak, and she coughed harshly.

"There's going to be a point in time when you have kids, and we both know you'll be a great mom. It'll be a point in time when you'll be truly happy. But no matter when that time comes, babe, no matter how often you feel lost along the way, I want you to remember that I love you more than anything. If you can, let that be your strength. Hold on to the thought that I'm somewhere out there, I don't know where, and I'll watch over you."

She dried her eyes with a tissue. "And if you need to cry or vent or talk, then talk to me, and I will listen. I promise you I will listen, okay? You see this?" She held up the damp tissue and smiled sadly. "I swore to myself that I wouldn't cry. That I'd make it a little easier for you. But I guess I failed. Please, Bethany, don't be mad at me. But last night, when we let go of that floating lantern, you know what I wrote on the paper? I wrote, 'Please, let me die happily.' And now that you're watching this, that's exactly what happened."

Bethany gave a cry of anguish, but Savy's words carried on. "Lory said it was a matter of days before things would have become even worse. I didn't want to leave this world connected to all those machines, not able to speak or tell you how much I love you, how much I'll miss you. But now I get to do all that. And I get to fall asleep next to the most important, most perfect person in my life, the woman who made me truly happy."

Her smile lit up her face. "Please be brave, Bethany. Do it for us. I know you can. I've always believed in you. And please tell Joan and Lory and my family that I love them. I couldn't have done it without all of you. Take good care of Tigger and our bucket book. Maybe you can finish the last check box without me one day? Maybe you'll think of me when you visit Machu Picchu?"

The sadness was back on her face. "I love you, Bethany. Never forget. I'll always be with you."

Savannah smiled and blew a soft little kiss into the camera, and the video finished.

Bethany dropped the phone. She looked left. Looked right. Her face was wet, and her head was spinning.

Not knowing what to do, she put on her bathrobe again, then stepped outside the apartment, not wearing any shoes.

Mrs. McPherson was cleaning the hallway when their eyes met. She could see the old lady didn't need to ask what had happened. Her usually strong and cold features immediately turned soft, and she dropped her broom.

"C'mere, girl. Oh no… Oh, come here, sweetheart." And she hugged her and let her sob out loud. "It doesn't feel like it right now, but it's gonna be okay. It's gonna be okay. I promise. Shush."

Looking back, Bethany had never expected her old grumpy neighbor, of all people, to be the one comforting her in this moment. She had pictured the moment a million times. Where it would happen. How and when. What she would do. What she would say.

She had never pictured it like this.

She had known it was going to happen, and she understood; it was the way Savannah had wanted it. Her last day on earth had been a happy one, and her last night had been spent next to the woman she loved. But it didn't matter how much time she'd had to prepare for this, it made no difference. No one could have prepared Bethany for the pain she felt or for the terrible emptiness that suddenly filled her heart.

It was a feeling so powerful it could break her within seconds.

But she would get through this. She had promised Savannah that.

She'd get through this for her.

For them.

Savannah Cortez died on July 5, 2015.
Her ashes were spread on Machu Picchu.

Check.

# About AC Oswald

AC Oswald grew up in a small town in Germany and has always loved creating her own fantasy worlds. Now she is in her mid-twenties but still a total child at heart.

She makes a living as a German and English teacher who also happens to work as an editor in a small publishing house. When she's not teaching or editing, she watches Netflix with her girlfriend or writes her own stories.

Since she's a big Disney nerd, her favorite place on earth is Disneyland Paris. If she could, she'd grab her family, her laptop, and her pug and move there permanently.

# Other Books from Ylva Publishing

www.ylva-publishing.com

# Flinging It

**G Benson**

ISBN: 978-3-95533-682-0
Length: 376 pages (113,000 words)

Midwife Frazer and social worker Cora have always grated on each other's nerves, but they have to work together to start up a programme for at-risk parents. Soon, the unexpected happens: they tumble into an affair. However, Cora is married to their boss, and both know it needs to end. But what they have might turn out to be much more than just a little distraction.

# The Return

**Ana Matics**

ISBN: 978-3-95533-234-1
Length: 300 pages (85,000 words)

Near Haven is like any other fishing village dotting the Maine coastline—a crusty remnant of an industry long gone, mired in sadness and longing. Liza thought she'd gotten out, escaped on a basketball scholarship, but a series of bad decisions has her returning home after a decade. She struggles to accept her place in this small town, making amends to people she's wronged and rebuilding her life.

# Rewriting the Ending
## hp tune

ISBN: 978-3-95533-503-8
Length: 286 pages (107,000 words)

Juliet is an author with a deadline. A big deadline…and a ratty old backpack, and she's on her way to Belgium.

Mia has a one-way, first class ticket to anywhere. Today anywhere happens to be Scotland. The one thing she knows is that money can't buy happiness, and she has no idea what does.

A chance meeting in an airport lounge and a shared flight itinerary leaves Juliet and Mia connected. They've known each other for only twenty-four hours and they are destined for separate countries. How do you forge a future when the past keeps pulling you back?

# Drawn Together
## JD Glass

ISBN: 978-3-95533-789-6
Length: 244 pages (80,000 words)

Zoe Glenn Edwards, graphic novelist, is determinedly single and happily married to her work. Dion Richards, author, is trapped in a hostile sham marriage and only happy when she's working. Both creatives are well-known in their respective fields. When they inevitably collaborate on a new project, what happens when two "unavailables" discover they're unmistakably Drawn Together?

Coming from Ylva Publishing

www.ylva-publishing.com

# Benched

*(The Love and Law Series - Book 2)*
**Blythe Rippon**

On the heels of their win for same-sex marriage equality, Supreme Court Justice Victoria Willoughby and LGBTQ rights lawyer Genevieve Fornier are thrust into the spotlight again. A photo of them almost kissing rocks their careers and new relationship, just as a same-sex parental law heads to court.

# Break Apart

**Meg Harrington**

Trauma surgeon Elle Matthews had a great thing going in San Antonio until a new colleague convinces her to get closer to her very straight crush, Doctor Kate Low.

Kate loves her husband and three children, even though he has grown distant after returning from Iraq.

Could her burgeoning friendship with Elle turn into love—a love that could break apart her marriage?

*Hold My Hand*
© 2017 by AC Oswald

ISBN: 978-3-95533-686-8

Also available as e-book.

Published by Ylva Publishing, legal entity of Ylva Verlag, e.Kfr.
Ylva Verlag, e.Kfr.
Owner: Astrid Ohletz
Am Kirschgarten 2
65830 Kriftel
Germany

www.ylva-publishing.com

First edition: 2017

Credits
Edited by Gill McKnight & Michelle Aguilar
Proofread by Joanie Bassler
Cover Design & Print Layout by Streetlight Graphics